Return of the Reich

Novella - PATH series

Robert A Webster

This book was professionally typeset on Reedsy.
Find out more at reedsy.com

Contents

1

The greater the lie, the greater the chance that it will be believed

Cheers and Jubilation erupting from the war-weary populous of Europe echoed around the world. The Second World War was over.

While liberated countries, now free of the brutal Nazi regime celebrated in the streets, German towns and cities lay in ruins.

With everybody believing the news that the tyrannical dictator and his young wife had committed suicide, the pair made their elaborate escape.

* * *

With thunderous explosions no longer reigning down from the roar of aircraft engines filling the skies, the air felt still.

Apart from the creaking and groaning of twisting metal, the

harbour and dockyard fell silent.

The man gazed into the distance at the crater-filled scorched earth on the hills surrounding this once scenic landscape. As cordite and diesel lingered in the air, he tugged the scarf covering his mouth and nose.

Rage burned in his eyes as he saw glistening black oil slicks rippling on the ocean's surface around the smouldering wrecks of his decimated fleet.

Although enraged by his defeat, Hitler knew this would not be the end of his plans for a new world order and his new Reich would rise from the ashes.

With seagulls screeching in the cloudy sky above, he swept his fringe over his forehead, pierced his lips, glowered, and strode up the gangway of the prototype U-boat, cursing. "Humanity will pay for this."

The sleek, black rubber-coated vessel slewed away from the crater-filled stone jetty, glided through the harbour, and submerged under the cold grey North Sea.

2

Great liars are also great magicians

A periscope sliced through the dark waters of the South Atlantic Ocean.

With his target in sight, the battle-weary haggard Kapitänleutnant Karl Viktor surfaced the U-boat.

Seawater hissed from the ballast tanks as the U-boat surfaced and steamed towards its rendezvous with the brightly lit crane barge.

Captain Viktor knew they were now in safe waters, with the Chilean navy that patrolled the Rio de la Plate area expecting them.

He went up cold metal rungs to the conning tower controls, took a deep breath of fresh air, removed his cap, and let the gentle sea breeze blow across his greasy blonde hair. He stroked the vulcanised rubber coating of his sleek vessel as he guided it alongside the barges port side, adjusting the U-boats buoyancy until the decks aligned, and the barge's crew tethered the vessels together.

* * *

The voyage had taken sixteen days without incident and although Captain Viktor had seen several allied battleships through the periscope, the undetectable electric-powered U-boat glided beneath them. He'd felt on edge after Hans Kruger, the SS commander, gave him orders and course headings at varying intervals, so until he received the final coordinates, neither he nor his crew knew their destination or their passengers.

Throughout the voyage, SS Commandos guarded the crew, either at their workstations or in their cramped, humid sleeping quarters, making communication between them difficult.

* * *

On a warm night and in calm seas, the vessels nudged against each other's mooring buoys.

The Captain turned on the U-boats deck lights as a crane boom swung above his head taking up position above one of the cargo hold sections.

Captain Viktor then heard a small engine, and looking amidships, he saw a wooden motor launch come from the port side of the barge and manoeuvre alongside the U-boat. He saw four SS Commandos come from the conning tower side hatch and removed a gangway from the U-boats deck, placing it on the hatchway to the open passenger section of the stylish motor launch.

The deck hatches opened and Captain Viktor smiled down

at his crew who looked relieved to be out in the fresh air. They ambled around the deck laughing and joking, but their joy didn't last as armed SS Commandos on the deck ordered them back inside and to their stations.

Captain Viktor sighed as he watched the Chilean barge crew swinging heavy lights around, bathing the U-boat's cargo section and conning tower in artificial sunlight. Several of the barge's crew jumped onto the U-boats deck as the crane lowered its lines.

After the crew attached the hooks, the crane hoisted a large square container section out of the U-boat. The Captain watched the crane boom swing the heavy load and deposited the cargo on the barge's deck, rocking the barge under its weight.

The Captain, leaning on the side of the conning tower, looked at his watch. It was 03:30, and according to his orders, after the offload was complete, he would then sail into US-controlled waters and surrender his U-boat to the allied fleet.

Captain Viktor realised when he saw the orders they were a bluff, he knew the Nazi regime would never allow him or his crew to live or the U-Boat to fall into enemy hands.

Knowing they were in 40 metres of water, he knew it was deep enough for them to disappear without a trace. He pierced his lips, looked down at the conning tower hatch, and gasped.

Hans Kruger stepped out of the side door of the conning tower and escorted the male and female passengers down the gangway onto the motor launch.

The man swept the fringe from his forehead, looked up at the Captain, and then spoke to Kruger, who smiled and nodded.

The Captain couldn't hear what orders Hans then gave to his Commandos before he boarded the launch, which pulled away from the U-boat.

That was the first time Captain Viktor had seen his mysterious guests and now knew that his crew and vessel were doomed. 'They aren't concerned about us seeing the Führer or the looted treasure because they know none of us will live to tell,' he thought.

The SS Commandos on deck watched the motor launch pull away while they stood on the gangway. Captain Viktor saw the crane boom get into position to hoist the next load out of his U-boat. He called the first officer to the conning bridge through the intercom pipe.

The XO, executive Officer, Oberleutnant Zur See, Johan Landis, came up and told the Captain that two SS Commandos were in the control room. Captain Viktor, knowing they couldn't be overheard, told the XO of his concerns and plan.

The XO sighed, and rubbing his hand across the stubble on his face, looked into the blue eyes of the weary Captain and shook his head. "No sir, that's suicide; we need to come up with an alternative."

"There's no time XO. We must act fast, I believe the SS have planted explosives, and I am prepared to take the risk." The Captain put his hand on the XO's shoulder, looked into his eyes, and with a rasp in his voice said. "You must let the world know the monster still lives."

The pair went below into the control room, closing the conning tower hatch above them. Captain Viktor spoke to the two SS guards, while the XO went to helm control, whispered to the helmsman, and then went to the engine order telegraph and pushed the lever to Stand By.

"What's happening?" asked a Commando, noticing the engine noise increase.

The Captain smiled and said. "Oh, it's nothing to worry about, we have to vent peroxide and recharge the batteries. This is the first surface recharge, so I have to go to the engine room to check the snorkel for our return voyage."

The Commando smiled, deciding to humour the Captain and allow him to continue believing they would go home.

The Captain sighed, furrowed his brow, scratched his head, and said. "But it will take a few men to lift and check the snorkel equipment. It is a simple job, but the chief engineer hurt his back." The Captain smiled at the Commando. "With the rest of the crew ordered to stay at their posts by SS-OberFührer Kruger, I don't know what to do," said the captain, throwing out his hands, and shrugging.

The muscular, stern-faced German SS Commando stared at him. "Okay, we'll come with you and help."

The Captain spun the wheel on the hatch to open the water-tight door, and he and the Commandos left the control room before the XO locked the hatch behind them.

"What's happening sir?" asked the Dive officer.

The XO sighed and told the crew what was about to happen, so be prepared.

The crew gasped.

"That's suicide sir," said the weapons officer looking shocked.

The XO sighed, nodded, and snapped. "Yes, I am well aware of that, so is the Captain."

The XO went to the hatch, jammed a wrench in the locking wheel, and looked through the small glass spy-port.

He saw Captain Viktor looking outside the conning tower hatch at the SS Commandos on deck.

"God be with you, my friend," mumbled the XO who continued to watch.

"What are you doing?" yelled one of the SS Commandos inside

who glared and then aimed his weapon at the captain who was now pulling the conning tower hatch shut.

"Stop!" yelled the other Commando, also aiming his weapon at the Captain who was turning the locking wheel.

The Captain turned and faced the Commandos. He grinned, lunged at the first Commando, and grabbed the muzzle of his machine gun.

When the XO saw the scuffle, he yelled. "Full-ahead!"

The coxswain pushed the lever to full-ahead. Seconds later, the engines revved up and the U-boat moved forward.

The Commando grappled with the Captain and with his superior strength and fighting skills easily subdued him, smashing his gunstock into his face, knocking him to the deck.

Captain Karl Viktor sat bloodied on the deck, laughing as the Commandos unlocked the conning tower hatch and pushed it open.

Pandemonium broke out on the surface when the submarine edged forward and the tether ropes strained as the crane barge got dragged along. The barge's Captain, feeling his boat judder and then move, panicked, and shouted orders to his crew to release or cut all moorings.

As the tightening mooring lines snapped or cut, the U-boat lurched forward, throwing the SS Commandos on deck into the frigid South Atlantic along with several Chilean crew from the U-boats deck.

The SS Commandos inside the conning tower rushed onto the deck as the U-boat edged forward, scraping along the side of the crane barge. Unable to see their comrades in the dark, they could only hear their screams, along with several Chilean crews splashing in the cold dark ocean, caught in the submarine's wake.

The two Commandos rushed back inside the conning tower looking bewildered. They glared at the Captain laughing on the floor with blood streaming down his face.

"Stop the boat!" yelled a Commando, his voice quivering. "Now," he said, aiming his weapon at the Captain's head.

"Of course," said Captain Viktor grinning. He stood up, spat blood and teeth onto the deck, went over to the spy-port in the control bridge door, looked at the XO, smiled, and mouthed an order.

The XO knew that with the side conning tower hatch open, they could dive the boat, but he wasn't sure they would have enough watertight integrity to re-surface.

He looked at the crew, who looked nervous as they awaited his order.

'At least we die like warriors,' he thought, and looked back at the Captain through the spy-port, smiled, nodded, and gave the order. "Dive the boat! Bow planes down 10 degrees, partial blow on main ballast, rapid descent."

He looked back through the spy-port and saw the captain standing against a bulkhead talking to the SS Commandos. The Captain was smiling as the U-boat dived and water rushed in through the open hatchway, gushing into the conning tower compartment. One Commando hurried over to close the hatch while the other fired a bullet into Captain Viktor's chest.

The XO watched in horror as the Captain fell forward and the Commando aimed at the spy-port as water gushed into the compartment.

The XO moved away expecting to see bullets shatter the small glass plate, but shots never came.

He looked again through the spy-port and saw the SS struggling against the pressure of the incoming torrent of freezing water as they tried to pull the hatch of the semi-flooded conning tower shut.

The compartment soon filled and the two soldiers gave up their futile attempts as their lungs filled with water and the XO watched their bodies convulsing as they drowned.

Landis saw the body of Captain Viktor swirling around in the cold seawater and put his forehead against the cold spy-port with sorrow in his eyes.

With extra ballast tanks fitted to carry the weight of the heavy cargo, and although the crew struggled with the sluggish con-trols, the U-boat broke the surface mid-afternoon.

In calm seas, the relieved crew boarded rubber life rafts and rowed away from the U-boat, which sank below the waves to its final resting depth at 130 metres.

The crew had opened the U-boats valves and flooded its ballasts tanks before abandoning the vessel, and after finding the SS's explosives in the forward torpedo room, they set the timers.

An eruption underwater sent plumes of black stained ocean skyward close to their position, drenching the crew in seawater and oil. The ocean calmed, and the XO smiled. "We won't be adrift long. I saw the ship on this heading through the periscope."

The crew nodded and sat silently in the bobbing rafts awaiting rescue.

"There they are sir!" exclaimed a crewman, pointing at three rubber rafts in the distance with their crews waving frantically back at him.

The XO looked relieved. "They've seen us men," he said, pointing at the small grey vessel approaching. A cheer erupted from his elated, dishevelled crew, caked in urine colour oil-stained seawater. He smiled. "We are going home," he breathed a sigh of relief, "our brave Captain did not die in vain, we can now let the world know."

The Chilean Captain sneered as he stood on the deck and looked through his binoculars. He grinned when he thought about the bounty in gold offered to him and his crew if they found their target and completed their mission. He glared at the crew. "You know what to do."

"Yes sir," said a crewman as he and the rest of the crew cocked their weapons.

3

For there is one thing we must never forget... the majority can never replace the man.

With several Fokker Kolibri helicopters outside and no roads or tracks, the concrete building looked out of place in the centre of acres of fenced land stretching kilometres in the barren wilderness, 400 kilometres east of Santiago.

Communications masts and aerials jutted from the buildings with cables extending as far as the eye could see.

On a mild winter's day, the air around the grounds surrounding the building shimmered as the land warmed by the heat from the bunker below.

A red Nazi flag hung on the wall of a large room behind a desk with a red telephone on one corner and a wooden chest placed at its centre. The red chest had a swastika symbol painted on each side, with writing stencilled across the top.

In the centre of the room, four people sat on armchairs around a large coffee table. The main entrance to this drawing-room within the bunker was from double doors opposite. Two armed SS soldiers stood outside while another soldier stood inside at a well-stocked drinks cabinet. The soldiers snapped to attention when three men dressed in pinstriped suits entered the room.

Adolf Hitler got off his chair and smiled at the newcomers who had escaped Germany years earlier.

The three men looked at their now frail, gaunt leader, but still saw the fire burning in his eyes that had beguiled a nation and brought a continent to its knees, with the menace in his voice still making them tremble.

"Welcome gentlemen, it has been a long time. I am pleased you got here safely. Now we can proceed with our plans for our new Reich."

Already seated in the room with Hitler were his wife, Eva, Hans Kruger, Hitler's ruthless Leibstandarte SS, personal bodyguard/ assassin, and a small, dark-haired middle-aged man.

Hitler instructed the newcomers to sit and offered them a drink.

The guard placed drinks on the table in front of the men and woman and then left the room.

Hitler sat back in his chair and smirked. "From the reports I received, the world has forgotten about me over the years. The fools believed our story when they found the incinerated corpses of our altered Jews."

"Yes Füehrer, although they caught and executed many of our party leaders, they are more concerned with the cold war and building their defences," said former Gestapo Chief, Heinrich Müller, removing maps from his case and laying them on the table.

Hitler looked at his wife who nodded, smiled, and sipped Gin and tonic.

Hitler then pointed to an area marked on the map and asked. "You are sure there are no others in this area?"

Múller looked at Hitler and replied, "Yes Füehrer, I am positive."

Hitler looked over at the chisel-jawed, middle-aged Hans Kruger and asked. "Is everything prepared, Hans?"

Hans Kruger sat upright, staring straight ahead. "Yes my Füehrer, my team is ready and awaiting your order."

Hitler looked at the map, smiled, and addressed the smaller man. "Erik, you have done well finding this. Are you prepared?"

"Yes, my Füehrer, everything has been taken care of," said the little man, smirking.

Hitler smiled and asked. "How do you know it will work Erik?"

The man pushed his wire-rimmed spectacles further up the bridge of his nose, smiled, and with an air of confidence, said. "I am sure Füehrer."

This small man seemed not to hold any fear of Adolf Hitler, which puzzled the military men in the room. They all had the same lingering doubts about Erik Jan Hanussen during the war.

Hitler was a staunch anti-Semitic, so they wondered why this Jew always stayed close to their Führer who would always listen to his advice, more so than any other of his war chiefs. They could not understand their close relationship, which was more of equals, as opposed to the reality of master and servant. Erik unnerved them all with his sinister and creepy demeanour.

Hitler studied the plans and the markings of a small valley alongside a glacial stream near the town of Schenkenzell, in the Kinzigtal valley at the edge of the Black Forest.

"Make sure you don't slow them down Erik," said Hitler, who smiled at Erik Jan Hanussen, his 'Jewish psychic.'

Erik smiled back, and looking nervous, glanced up at Hans Kruger sat next to him. "No my Füehrer, I will try not to," he stammered as Hans gave him an icy stare.

"Kruger, make sure no harm befalls Erik. The Reich's continuing existence and future 1,000-year reign rest on his shoulders," said Hitler, glaring at Hans.

"I will take good care of Herr Jan Hanussen, My Füehrer," said Hans, smirking at Erik.

"You have your orders, so carry them out. Failure is not an option and will result in your death, Kruger," said Hitler, with a menace in his voice.

The two stood and Hans saluted Hitler before marching out of the room with Erik stumbling behind him.

Müller smiled and said. "Once Kruger completed his mission, we can start again. Your Reich will once again be the world's superior power under your leadership and guidance, my Füehrer."

Hitler smirked, knowing only Eric would be there to witness the new Reich. Müller and everyone involved would be long dead. "Thank you Heinrich, take some gold on your way out to help with your expenses... and don't get caught."

Heinrich smiled, saluted, left the room, and went to the bullion store.

After loading up his duffel bag with gold ingots, he and his pilot went up the elevator to the building on the surface and flew off in one helicopter.

Hitler then turned his attention to the two men remaining in the room with him and Eva, who looked nervous.

"How is Argentina Josef?" he asked former S.S. Hauptsturm-Führer Doctor Josef Mengele, the angel of death.

"Fine my Füehrer, but I miss Germany," said Josef sweeping back his greying hair.

Hitler nodded and turned to face Professor Kurt Gutzieg. "How are you and your family, Kurt, where are you hiding... Oh, excuse me gentlemen," said Hitler as the phone on his desk rang.

Hitler answered the call that he was expecting from SS-Obersturmbannfüehrer, Adolf Eichmann.

Hitler got straight to the point and snapped. "Why aren't you here? Has everything gone according to plan Eichmann?"

Eichmann replied, and the three saw Hitler becoming irate as he yelled. "That is no excuse. You are already years behind schedule. What do you mean 90% complete? Are they dead?"

Again, Eichmann replied, and after giving details, Hitler said, "So, the result is, 100% of the 500 unprotected test subjects died, but it affected none of the 20 immunised individuals?" Hitler calmed down, smiled, and said, "Eichmann, that sounded like a 100% success."

Eichmann then told him that he needed time to work on an airborne delivery system and the Triad wanted more gold to provide Chinese peasants for experimenting on at their facility near Beijing.

Hitler, trembling with rage, thundered. "We have no time for that. I must get this information immediately," and with menace in his voice, said, "we can leave those details for the future. You must get here with all haste Eichmann, do I make myself clear."

Hitler glared at the phone, unnerving the three in the room. He panted like an enraged bull and then calmed down as he swept his grey fringe from his forehead. "What about the other scientists and the surviving test subjects, are they with you now?" he calmly asked.

"Yes Füehrer," Eichmann confirmed, "they are here, along with the Triad assassins as ordered."

"Get here as soon as you can Eichmann. I am waiting, and you know what you must do?" said Hitler and with a sinister tone to his voice, added, "leave no trace Eichmann... do you understand?"

Hitler heard Adolf Eichmann issue an order in Chinese, and the sound of automatic gunfire reverberated through the telephone.

He smirked, hung up, and went back over and sat with the three. They had overheard the end of the call, which sent a chill through both the medical academics as Eva smirked.

Professor Kurt Gutzieg's hands quivered as he took five buff coloured folders from his case and placed them on the coffee table.

Mengele moved three thin folders to one side and said. "Those are the three who did not survive after the allies took Berlin."

He picked up two thicker folders and handed them to Hitler, who opened one folder and took out A4 size documents with photographs.

Hitler looked like a proud father as he showed the photographs to Eva.

Eva had tears in her eyes when she looked at each image and smiled at the small black and white photographs of mothers cradling newborn infants, with larger colour ones of the boys taken several years later.

Kurt Gutzieg then smiled and said. "This process I named Gutzieg Esterne Ovarielien Inseminatin, and as you can see it has been a great success." He was about to explain his technique when Hitler abruptly cut him off.

"Have you any other copies of this technique?"

"Yes, Füehrer," said Kurt, looking confused as he reached into his case and took out a file and a small journal. "All my research is in that file and my journal.

"Anything else?" Hitler asked, glaring at the Professor.

"No Füehrer," said Gutzieg, furrowing his brow and looking nervous.

Hitler held out his hand, and the Professor handed him his journal, assuming he wanted to study it.

Hitler went over to a circular tin bin, dropped the file and journal inside, and doused them with lighter fuel.

Noticing the shocked expression and disbelief on Professor Gutzieg's face, he said. "If this fell into the wrong hands, they would realise we have done something using this technique and investigate your work, and we can't allow that... can we Kurt?"

Hitler dropped a lit match into the bin, igniting the papers.

Gutzieg watched his work ablaze. He sighed, shook his head, and sounding hoarse, said. "No, my Füehrer."

Hitler sat and glared at Mengele. "Are you familiar with the Professor's technique, Josef?"

Mengele had known Hitler for some time, so became suspicious of his question.

"No Füehrer, I have never been involved in the Professor's research, I only performed the insemination with the frozen embryos' Kurt provided."

Kurt Gutzieg looked shocked by Mengele's reply, because he had spent a great deal of time assisting him and knew his techniques, so why lie? A horrifying thought then entered his mind. He felt nauseous and afraid as Mengele, changing the subject, said. "The two surviving mothers and children are in excellent health."

Hitler scowled at the Doctor. "Are you certain they don't know what happened?"

Mengele nodded. "Positive Füehrer; I inseminated them all during routine operations."

Hitler smirked. "Kurt, you performed all these embryo implant techniques?"

Feeling numb with shock, Gutzieg replied. "Yes Füehrer." He glared at Mengele and told Hitler, "I performed yours and Eva's egg fertilisation," although he felt unsure why he should protect Mengele.

Hitler took all the folders from the table, went over to the wooden chest, and unlocked it. When he lifted the lid, he shouted over at the two men. "You've destroyed any samples?"

"Yes Füehrer, I destroyed everything as per your orders," said Mengele sneering.

Hitler put the files into the red chest, closed the lid, slipped on a thick padlock, and re-joined the sitting group. Eva was still smiling, unaware of the fate of one of the two men who sat beside her.

"Thank you gentlemen... that will be all... Josef, Keep me informed of their progress," said Hitler and summoned the guards.

"I will take care of that personally Füehrer," said Mengele as two guards came over and Hitler spoke to one, who then glared at Kurt Gutzieg.

Gutzieg and Mengele stood.

Gutzieg trembled and Mengele smirked as Hitler ordered. "Take the Doctor and Professor topside and make sure they are well taken care of before they leave."

The soldiers snapped to attention and escorted the two out of the room.

Gutzieg dawdled, terrified of his impending doom. He was a proud man and even though he knew he would never see his family again, he accepted his fate with dignity.

He glanced back at Hitler who now had his back turned while

he spoke to Eva.

Gutzieg saw the embers of his life's work smouldering within the dying flames in the bin and sighed.

"Herr Professor, please come this way," said the guard as he lagged behind Mengele and his escort.

* * *

On a fresh, crisp, spring morning in the Kinzigtal alpine valley, white smoke billowed out of the chimney stack of an isolated white Nordic stone cottage. A pleasant aroma from the cottage drifted on the breeze as Twigg Hansen and his wife, Freda, prepared their meals for the day. Bread baking in the wood-fired oven gave the cottage and surroundings a homely smell.

Twigg and Freda lived at the cottage with their baby son, Ulrich. Twigg worked his land and took care of livestock while Freda took care of Ulrich and household chores. She visited the nearby town of Schenkenzell on occasions if a resident who lived there had a spiritual problem that Freda could help with. Their secluded, simple life was idyllic, far different from the rest of their war-torn country. This homestead and the Hansen Clan had survived untouched and unhindered for generations... until now.

Twigg and Freda had finished eating breakfast when an invisible force shocked the couple, sending a cold chill through them both. Twigg was a tall, well-built German man with long blonde hair and piercing blue eyes. It seemed hard to imagine that anything could put fear into this individual, but something had.

Twigg went outside feeling foreboding and looked up.

He saw large round parachutes with men and equipment drifting down from an aeroplane.

Twigg watched as they neared the ground and one caught his attention. He gasped when he saw the man's cobalt blue aura and rushed inside.

Hans Kruger and his Commandos landed on an alpine meadow surrounding the cottage, removed their parachutes, and while Kruger waited for the last man to land, the others went to check the large crates dropped with them.

Kruger helped the clumsy man remove his parachute. The shocked looking Jewish man trembled, took his spectacles from his pocket, and nodded at Kruger as he put on and adjusted his glasses.

Kruger cocked his machine gun as he looked down and smirked at Eric. "Wait here," he ordered.

4

If you want to shine like the sun, first you have to burn like it.

"Church, Church… are you okay!" yelled Ryan rushing over and shaking the Keeper's shoulders.

Church, dazed, squinted at Ryan and then around the room. He wiped vomit from around his mouth with his hand as his faculties returned.

Composing himself but seeming unaware of his surroundings, Church put his cluttered desk in order.

Ryan stood back and watched as colour returned to Church's ashen face and he'd stopped trembling. "That was a powerful one boss; Pinky and I felt it in the living room."

Church coughed, focusing on Ryan, and with a quake in his voice, said. "That was the worst experience and the most powerful Spirit that I have ever encountered."

Ryan frowned. "What was it?" he asked, but the answer never came.

The door swung open, and a young woman with short blonde hair entered the room carrying two mugs. She went over to

Church and Ryan.

"Are you okay, Church?" asked Pinky sounding concerned as she handed both men a mug of tea and said. "Here, drink this."

"Thanks, but I need something stronger than tea Pinky," said Church, his hands trembling as he took the mug.

"I know, so I put a drop of Johnny Walker in it," said Pinky and smiled.

"Great!" exclaimed Ryan, who after slurping his tea, winced.

"Duh, not for you, dopey," said Pinky and chuckled.

Church looked around the Spirit room, which looked like a tornado had blown through their secluded white stone-cottage within a forest on the Yorkshire Moors.

Church drank his beverage and felt the whisky hit the back of his throat and caressing his oesophagus as it eased down, giving him a warm glow. He exhaled, picked up his notepad, glanced at it, and then put it on the desk.

Ryan picked up the notepad, read Church's scribblings, and tutted. "Hmm, you've written them in bloody German."

Pinky went to the sink, brought over a damp flannel, and wiped Church's face.

Church looked at the two mortal Spirit Guides, his team, and family.

Pinky gasped and pointed. "Whatever it was, it scorched the wall behind the Portal."

Church took another sip of tea and nodded. "It was a Diabolus. I know about these demons from the Potts journal. It is not the first time one has entered our Portal," he said and shuddered.

"I can't smell brussels sprouts. Where was Granny Pearl? Why did she not come to help?"

Church quivered and then shook his head. "I don't know Ryan, and that's what concerns me. If this powerful demon so easily overpowered me, perhaps it did the same to our Spirit Keeper and Guide before it came through our Portal."

Pinky picked Church's smartphone off the floor, handed it to him, and asked. "What would be powerful enough to do that?" she then chuckled, "and why pick on our Yorkshire Bob Hoskins look-a-like? You should have set t' ferret on it," she said, mimicking Church's Yorkshire brogue.

Church smiled, focused on the small phone keypad, typed in instructions, and an image came on screen.

"He would!" exclaimed Church, showing them the phone.

Pinky and Ryan gasped when they saw the image and Ryan furrowed his brow. "That explains why your Spirit notes are in German, but he's been dead over seventy years; shouldn't he be tucked away in the afterlife?"

Church shrugged. "I don't understand either Ryan, we need Granny Pearl here, perhaps she can explain."

While Church read his Spirit notes with the instructions given to him by the demon, Ryan and Pinky righted the overturned furnishings in the Spirit room.

A surreal silence lingered in the room as the clanging chimes of doom rang in the PATH teams heads as the three powerful psychics wondered what could have happened in the Spirit World.

Churchill Potts, the mortal Keeper of the Potts Portal, felt concerned for his Spirit Keeper and her Spirit Guide, his deceased grandparents, Pearl and Jack Potts.

From when he was eighteen, his grandparents had taught the now middle-aged Church about the Spirit World and his duty as the Portal Keeper.

He had read the ancient Potts journal many times and, although it mentioned a Diabolus Spirit entering the Potts Portal over 400 years earlier, with it being so long ago, he hadn't paid it much heed.

However, nothing he had read or been taught could have prepared him for his encounter with the powerful demon.

Although brief, the confrontation confused Church as the dark demon gave off no aroma and had a black aura; with its power so intense, Church felt the air sucked out of the room, making his head spin before he vomited.

Concerned, he looked at the youngest member of the PATH team, Pinky, washing the scorch marks off the wall.

Church thought how much this young woman resembled her dead auntie, Heidi, with her porcelain complexion, piercing blue eyes, and an angelic face. However, she cursed and swore like a Grimsby fishwife with a Danish twang when riled, especially at Ryan.

Several years earlier, after her death, Heidi, now a Spirit Guide, had asked Church to rescue her niece.

Sharon Pinquist's parents had kept her locked away like an insane child, mistaking the frightened teenager's powerful psychic gift as madness. They would have had her institutionalised if not for the government benefits they received as her registered carers. Church made her greedy parents an offer they readily accepted and Pinky moved to the cottage and became his mortal guide and apprentice.

Church then looked at the ever-hungry Ryan, the last member to join the team. He chuckled when he recalled how many times Pinky had bollocked him for raiding the fridge.

Previously a professional boxer, Ryan had attained his psychic gift by accident. Granny Pearl asked Church and Pinky to meet him, explain his gift, and reassure him. Ryan felt afraid and uncertain of his gift at first and with his boxing career over, Church asked the confused young man to join him and Pinky in the PATH team.

His crooked nose, muscular build, and cockney accent came in useful while the Paranormal Assisted Treasure Hunters conducted their edict.

They found treasures hidden by restless Spirits during their lifetime and gave them to their disbelieving and sometimes suspicious families, so the Spirit would find peace and cross over to the afterlife.

Although a powerful Keeper, Church, feeling anxious, rubbed his chin and furrowed his brow. "Why would this Diabolus want us to find it and take something to its son? I wasn't aware he had any children in his lifetime," he shuddered when recalling the power he had felt. He then smiled and looked relieved as he spun around to face the Portal as the smell of brussels sprouts and Brylcreem filled the air.

Pinky and Ryan stopped what they were doing. They turned and looked at the circle on the wooden floor surrounded by a Pentagram in the corner of the room.

Church saw the Portal filling with a rainbow of intense light as Pinky and Ryan sniffed the air.

"Great," said Ryan, raising his eyebrows. "Granny Pearl and Grandpa Jack's here so maybe we can get some answers."

5

Keep a very firm grasp on reality, so you can strangle it at any time.

Church, still shaken when Granny Pearl and Grandpa Jack appeared in the portal, and Granny Pearl's voice trembled when she asked. "Are you okay, Church?"

"I am now," said Church, "but I don't know what happened. That was the worst experience ever. Why weren't you here and what has taken you so long to come?"

"I'm sorry Church, but with Spirit Guides searching for the Diabolus when it entered the Spirit World I was alone at the portal when it attacked me. It drained my energy and by the time help arrived it had gone."

Church felt rage from his Spirit Guide, Grandpa Jack, and they all heard the anger in his voice as he mumbled about getting hold of the demon and kicking its arse as Granny Pearl asked. "What did it want?"

Church explained and felt confusion coming from his Spirit guardians.

"Hmm," mumbled Granny Pearl. "You must follow its instructions so we can find it."

A chill went down Church's spine and his grandparents picked up his fear.

"I know you are afraid my grandson, but not only do you have a powerful gift Church, but you are the only team we have capable of fighting the demon."

"What? You mean we are the only hope for the survival of the Spirit World. The Fantastic Three... Cool," chuckled Ryan.

"No Ryan. You are the only hope for the survival of Your world," said Granny Pearl, and after giving the team further instructions, she and Grandpa Jack vanished, leaving the team looking shocked and feeling confused.

* * *

After the visit by Granny Pearl and Grandpa Jack, and with their investigation underway, Pinky glanced at news coverage on TV while crafting the items as Granny Pearl instructed.

"I still don't understand how the Spirit World lost the Hansen's Portal years ago," she said looking confused.

"What?" asked Church, who, although reading the Potts journal by the computer, his thoughts were preoccupied with the news Granny Pearl gave them. He felt concerned how the Diabolus had easily overpowered his Spirit Keeper and him, along with the emotions of fear and uncertainty he had felt from his Spirit Guardians.

Pinky repeated her question and Church said. "It's like Granny Pearl explained, Portals appear as many balls of light in the Spirit World, so if one closes, it's like a light being turned off in the vastness of space. Without the beacon of the Spirit Keeper's aura, the closed Portal would be impossible to trace within the Spirit World."

"But Granny Pearl said that it appeared again for an instant about forty-years-ago; the same time they said they detected a Diabolus in the Spirit World, but it vanished," said Ryan who sat chomping on a chicken drumstick.

Church nodded. "I think that's when Hitler must have died and become a Diabolus. They also believed the Hansens Portal was opened and closed for him and that's where he has been hiding."

"Opened by whom, and why has he now come out of hiding and contacted you."

Church shrugged. "We don't know who or what opened the Portal Ryan." He rubbed his chin and sounding wistful said, "I know the last Diabolus encounter in the Spirit World came through our Portal 400-years ago, so it must have left some kind of residue."

He tapped on the ancient Potts journal. "I read Joshua Potts entry on how he and his Spirit Guardians encountered the sixteenth century Diabolus of Adam Weishaupt S.J., a professor, Jesuit, mass-murderer, and founder of the Illuminati." Church furrowed his brow and looked confused. "But Joshua wrote that their Diabolus was the colour of the twilight sky, so it sounded like their demon was blue." Church shrugged, "but it mentioned nothing else about that, other than how they contained it and took it to the afterlife."

Ryan pointed to the TV. "Well, it seemed suspicious how he contacted you the same day as the American President suddenly dropped dead."

Pinky looked at the TV and then at Ryan smirking. "Don't be daft Ryan; according to his friend, the retired Secret Service

Director who was with him, he died of a heart attack. And that happened in America, so the Diabolus could have had nothing to do with that."

Pinky turned up the volume on the TV and the CNN broadcaster announced. "Vice President George Wolffe will be sworn into office later today as the Forty-Fifth President of the United States."

The screen showed pictures of the smiling Vice President on the White House lawn with his family.

Church furrowed his brow as a chill coursed through him. He looked at the face of the new President.

"Why did nobody notice that before?" asked Ryan, taken aback. "All he's missing is a hairy leach under his nose. Perhaps it's just a coincidence, but the likeness is uncanny,"

"Hmm," mumbled Church.

The team watched the broadcast and then Church turned down the volume and Pinky looked worried. "According to what they reported earlier, all they know about that bugger is that he's a war-monger with his hard-line, zero-tolerance policies, especially with foreign governments. They also said he helped plan Ronald Reagan's Star Wars project in the eighties and nineties."

"The Star Wars project; wasn't that about putting weapons in space?"

Church nodded. "I think it was something like that Ryan, but I am not sure."

Pinky then looked at Church and Ryan. "They said earlier that they have little information on him because it's rumoured any journalist who investigated him disappeared."

Church rubbed his chin and looked at his watch. "We can't concern ourselves with that now, let the Americans deal with that problem, we have our urgent matter to attend to. Hitler's Diabolus gave me scant information, only telling me that I needed to find a cottage where it would be waiting to give me further instructions."

Church touched his hibernated computer screen and a map with images he'd found earlier appeared. "At least the Diabolus gave me a starting point," he said pointing at the images, "I'll book three plane tickets and rooms for tomorrow. We can rent a car at the airport and stay in the town on the map. Hopefully, someone will know where the cottage is and give us directions."

6

Mankind grew strong through eternal struggle; it follows that he shall perish through eternal peace.

The Keepers dulled rainbow auras swirled slowly around the Portal.

Twigg Hansen and his Spirit Keeper father, conjoined in this Limbo decades ago by one of the Diabolus hovering back and forth inside a large glass room in the cellar, felt concerned.

Still drained after their recent overpowering confrontation, Twigg looked over at his wife and son's crimson Spirits swirling around their skeletons within their crystal coffin at the centre of a large glass room resembling a huge aquarium.

"Something evil's happening son," said Fritz. "Whatever Hitler and Jan Hanussen planned all those years ago before Jan Hanussen and his SS thugs trapped us in here and killed Freda and Ulrich in the coffin to keep us subdued, must be coming to fruition."

"I agree Father; why else would Hitler's demon risk going

past us again to the Spirit World other than to cause mayhem? Look how excited the Diaboluses now appeared." Twigg sighed, "but we are helpless to do anything, they are too powerful," he said sounding enraged, as the Diaboluses hovered around a red wooden chest in the glass room.

"Soon Eric, we will be out of this prison and with the help of Churchill Potts and my son, my Reich will once again dominate the planet," said a menacing voice from the swirling black mist.

"Excellent, so the American President's dead?" cackled Eric's cobalt blue Diabolus.

"Yes, I saw his Spirit on the way to the afterlife before I went to see Potts. Now my son is President, he will have the power of the world in the palms of his hands. He will be surprised and overjoyed to meet his real father and I will have my revenge."

Erik Jan Hanussen, not only Hitler's Jewish psychic when alive, but a powerful Diabolus ally in death, sniggered. "And you are certain Potts will come?" and with hope in its voice asked, "will he come alone?"

"Yes, he will come, he has no choice, and he will bring his two mortal Guides with him, so you will also have a vessel."

"Excellent, excellent... thank you, my Füehrer," said Eric's Diabolus pulsating with excitement.

"We can deliver the journal to my son as proof. It will impress him when we show him the weapon Eichmann developed which our colonies will launch on his order."

Hitler's Diabolus sneered. "With the help of my son, we can eliminate the weak human race in a single blow, leaving my protected Reich to fashion the new world to the Utopia that I ordained."

7

Never deprive someone of hope; it may be all they have

"And you're sure it's here?"

Church nodded. "According to the directions the townsfolk gave us yesterday it is Pinky... Yes, look."

With his hand on the steering wheel, Church pointed as they drove from the forest and saw a white-stone cottage in the alpine meadow a short distance away.

Wisps of smoke curling from the rustic cobbled-stoned chimney at the side made Pinky smile. "It's picturesque, just like our cottage on the Moors, and the crisp alpine air felt like an English autumn day."

"Ooh, I can smell fresh bread baking," said Ryan smirking with his head out of the back window as they neared the cottage.

Church felt trepidation as they drove up to the thick wooden door. He rubbed the metal talisman under his jacket that Granny Pearl and Grandpa Jack instructed them all to make and stopped the car. Fear coursed through him as he recalled his encounter with the Diabolus and he looked at Pinky and then back at a smiling Ryan.

"It doesn't look like the lair of an evil tyrant, but there must be someone here. I wonder if they will make me a sandwich, that fresh bread smells delicious."

"Can't you think about anything other than bloody food Ryan," said Pinky scolding him.

Ryan smirked. "How can we fight evil demons on an empty stomach? Besides, Granny Pearl and the other Spirits said they would monitor us and help once we found the location."

"Yeah," said Pinky sounding confident, "she said they would pop through temporary Portals and kick the demon's arse until we can fix the Hansen's Portal. Well, she might not have put it like that, but that's what she meant," she chuckled.

Although Church smiled and nodded, he knew this would not be that simple. He turned off the ignition and took a deep breath. "Okay team, let's go."

Pinky, Church, and Ryan got out of the car and approached the door. They stood back looking aghast when a large German man with a smile a mile wide opened it.

"Welcome, we have been expecting you," he said as a German woman with tightly bunched blonde hair and harsh features came and stood beside him. "I am Olaf, and this is my female companion, Hilda."

"What did they say?" whispered Pinky as only Church's Keepers gift gave him the ability to understand every language known.

Church smiled and introduced the team.

Olaf invited them into the warm homely cottage.

Ryan tapped his lips together and smirked when he saw a fresh crusty loaf, a large wedge of cheese, and a juicy ham hock on the thick wooden table.

"Our handler told us that you would arrive soon. We are honoured you came during our watch," said Hilda, looking excited and relieved.

"Would you like something to eat or would you prefer to go straight to the cellar," smiled Olaf.

"I would love a sandw..."

"No, we're fine," interrupted Church, "please, take us to the cellar."

Ryan sighed and broke off a chunk of cheese as Olaf and Hilda led them to a wooden door.

Olaf took a large key off a hook, turned on the old light switch, and opened the door.

The couple had been on duty at the cottage for two years. They'd always felt confused why they had to stand on the wooden gantry of the cold, damp cellar and read aloud any news article on certain subjects as ordered by their handler.

Their orders were never to go down the cellar, but several days ago, their handlers in Berlin told them to expect strangers, show them into the cellar, and when they returned, obey the stranger's instructions. The modern-day Nazi pair followed their orders without questions.

With Ryan chomping on the lump of cheese, the three walked a short distance along a small wooden gantry and stood at the top of the steps.

"We will await your return as instructed. Just knock and we will open the door... Heil Hitler," said Olaf snapping to attention and giving a Hitlergruss before locking the door behind them.

As the PATH team reached the bottom of the old wooden steps, Church gasped. His Keeper power enabled him to see auras and feel emotions of Spirits. Unlike Ryan and Pinky, whose Guides powers only allowed them to hear the Spirits and smell their unique aromas.

Church saw Twigg and Fritz's aura's swirling around the corner of the room. He furrowed his brow and looked confused at the floor when he saw a smudge. 'That was their pentagram protection. What the hell happened here?' he thought as Pinky coughed and gagged. "I can't breathe Church, and I feel dizzy," she croaked, choking as the air sucked out of the room and Ryan spat out his chewed lump of cheese as he struggled for air.

"Welcome Churchill Potts, and your friends," said a guttural voice from within a large glass room that sent a chill down Church's spine as he spun around.

Church's head spun as he glanced at the swirling dark mists hovering in the doorway of the glass room and they heard sniggering as the air returned to the cellar.

Church, Pinky and Ryan gasped, taking several lungs full of air as the room stopped spinning.

"A demonstration of my power, Keeper," snarled the Diabolus.

Pinky and Ryan looked at one another, both now able to understand the German-speaking demon.

Church focused on the quivering black and cobalt blue swirling human-shaped mists and his eyes widened. 'Two Diabolus!" he gasped and thought. 'That explained why the Portal disappeared and what opened it again years ago. The Spirit World don't know about this... damn. I must let them know what they are up against.' He then looked at the demonic symbols of concealment and protection glowing red on the glass walls.

He then saw two Spirit Guides Crimson auras in the crystal coffin in the centre of the room with demonic confinement symbols painted on the top.

Church trembled with fear, realising their situation. He knew he and his Spirit cavalry had underestimated this powerful demon's ability and cunning.

"Come in here Potts," ordered the black demon with a throaty roar, "I want you to open this chest and take the contents to my son."

Church glanced inside the glass room at the old red wooden chest with 'Buch Mose' stencilled in black along the top. He furrowed his brow and quivered, he knew that once in the glass room he would be vulnerable. He took a deep breath and felt his talisman.

"What are you waiting for Potts, come in here... now!"

Church then heard the sarcasm in the Diaboluses tone when he said. "Are you waiting for your puny Spirits to rescue you? Any attempt to defeat us will be futile. Now, come in here!"

"And bring the male Guide," said Eric's Diabolus, wanting to use Ryan as his vessel.

Ryan shuddered, although he had never been afraid of anyone, something in the demons menacing tone sent a shiver down his spine. He rubbed his amulet under his jacket and sounding defiant, snarled. "Piss off Kraut, if you want a fight, you can come out here."

Church felt concerned and afraid. He knew with the Portal closed any help would only come from temporary Portals and he looked at the symbols on the glass walls.

Church knew the energy the Spirits needed to create temporary Portals, along with the Diabolus' power amplified by the symbols; any help would only stay minutes before having to return to the Spirit World to rejuvenate.

"Very well Potts, if that's how you want it," said Hitler's Diabolus and its black aura flew out of the glass room and streaked towards Church.

"Now," shouted Church, and the three opened their jackets showing their amulets.

The Diabolus's stopped; Hitler's in front of Church and Eric's in front of Ryan.

Church heard the demon gasp and its aura dimmed for several seconds before it chuckled and flew into his mouth.

Church gagged before his body felt on fire. He slumped to the floor, as did Ryan, both convulsing as they fought a battle with the demons within. Church felt in limbo, with his essence bathed an intense white light with the large black orb of the Diabolus in front of his small Rainbow orb.

Pinky looked on trembling. She felt helpless until she smelt Granny Pearls brussels sprouts and Grandpa Jack's Brylcreem odour, along with several others as the Spirits joined the fray.

Unable to see anything, she yelled. "I think the demons are in Church and Ryan."

"We know Pinky," said Granny Pearl, "don't be afraid, we can help now."

The battle raged within Church as the Diabolus threw his soul around his inner being like a rag-doll. "Your vessel is mine Potts; accept your fate and leave. It will save you any more pain and your soul can go to your precious Spirit World."

"Never," said Church sounding defiant.

His Rainbow orb soul rushed again at the large black orb, only to be swatted away like an insect by the sniggering demon. Church knew his attempts were futile as he felt weaker with each assault.

Pinky, seeing Church's tremors easing, knew he was losing his cosmic internal battle.

Bursting into tears of frustration, she looked up. "Help him," she screamed, but there was no reply.

Church then felt a rush of energy as Spirit Keepers and Guides joined him. Seeing Rainbow and Crimson orbs flashing on and off and barging the black demon gave him renewed energy. He launched himself again at the demon and felt it weakening as its black orb faded and then vanished.

Church opened his eyes, much to the relief of Pinky, who helped him stand. He saw a myriad of bright Rainbow and Crimson lights appearing and disappearing outside the glass room. The Diabolus hovered back and forth inside the glass room cursing, and when it saw Church standing, it snarled. "This is only temporary, Keeper, and your power alone cannot defeat me... you will be mine."

Church looked down at Ryan shaking and convulsing on the floor, knowing the battle still raged within his young friend as Crimson and Rainbow orbs flew in to help.

"The Diabolus is correct Church; we can't keep them confined for long with temporary Portals. You need to open the Hansen's Portal," said Granny Pearl sounding anxious.

Church looked confused at his grandmother's Rainbow orb now stood beside him, and asked. "How do I do that Gran?"

Church then looked at Ryan, whose quivering body seemed to have taken on new energy as more angelic orbs flew into him.

"Go to the Portal son and hurry," said Grandpa Jacks Crimson orb sounding urgent.

While Pinky knelt beside Ryan urging him to fight, Church and the two orbs went over to the Portal.

The Hansen's auras pulsated, aware something was about to happen.

"Church, put your arm into the Portal," Granny Pearl instructed.

Church gasped and looked at her Rainbow orb. His eyebrows

rose and sounding shocked said. "But Gran, you told me a mortal Keeper and Spirit Keeper cannot be present in a Portal at the same time." He trembled and pointed at the intertwined Keepers. "That must be what happened to them, and what closed their Portal.

"You are correct," said Granny Pearl, "but this is not our Portal Church, and neither Grandpa Jack nor I am in there. Please Church, hurry."

Church looked, gulped, closed his eyes, and thrust his arm inside the swirling Rainbows and screamed as electricity coursed through him and he felt as if a fire crawled through him. He then breathed a sigh of relief as the pain stopped and shimmering rainbow orbs appeared by his side. Church felt the Hansen's emotions of freedom and gratitude before they entered the now empty Portal and vanished.

Church looked back toward the glass room and saw the Rainbow and Crimson orbs disappearing, so were the ones now coming from Ryan.

His grandparents' orbs also vanished, leaving Church afraid and confused. "What's happening?" He screamed aloud as the last orb vanished.

Looking shocked, he rushed over to Ryan and Pinky.

Pinky looked up at him with desperation written across her face as Ryan's body now lay still with the occasional spasm as Eric's Diabolus overwhelmed Ryan's soul.

"They've left Ryan to die," croaked Pinky as she held onto his hand and felt his life draining.

"Yes Potts, what did you expect? They can't defeat us, we are far too powerful," said the black Diabolus from the glass room and sniggered. "Now, where were we... ah yes... I was about to take my vessel."

Church looked down at Ryan and then glared at the Diabolus.

"I will give you my body, but make him stop and leave Ryan alone."

The Diabolus sneered. "You are in no position to make demands Potts. We will take you both and then kill the woman Guide, she isn't necessary."

"Fuck off idiot," snapped Pinky, gritting her teeth and scowling.

The Diabolus sniggered. "Hmm, feisty, when I get my vessel I will have fun with you before you die."

"You can try buster," snarled Pinky as the Diabolus came from the glass room and hovered over to Church.

"Now Potts, do you want to make this easy or hard? If you choose the easy route, I might allow the female Guide to live."

Church gulped, recalling his last battle with this powerful adversary but with a slim hope that it might spare Pinky, he nodded.

"Take off the amulet," snarled the Diabolus, "that will make it easier for me and less painful for you."

"Give me your word that you won't harm Pinky and I will not put up a fight."

"You have my word Potts, now take off the amulet," said the Diabolus and sniggered.

Church sighed, removed the amulet from around his neck, and handed it to Pinky.

"No Church," screamed Pinky looking distraught.

"I have no choice Pinks," said Church, looking into the frightened, tear-filled eyes of the girl he considered his daughter.

He then looked at Ryan's still body and knew his battle was almost lost. "I am sorry for getting you into this mess my young friend," he whispered.

Pinky juddered; she had never felt as helpless or afraid as she clung onto Church's amulet.

She then recalled what Granny Pearl had told them. 'You can never defeat this Diabolus alone. You need the combined power of the three of you, and these amulets will amplify your powers and protect you.'

While the demon gloated in front of Church, Pinky puckered her brow, took off her amulet, leant over, and removed Ryan's.

With the three amulets together in her hand, she felt a surge of energy and gasped... she could now see the black Diabolus.

The Diabolus stopped gloating and snarled. "Drop the amulets woman, or you will be sorry."

"Not as sorry as you, dickhead," she screamed as she stood up and thrust her hands into the shimmering black mist.

Pinky's hands felt on fire as the Diabolus yelled and backed away. Pinky, with her hands in the black mist, moved forward, forcing the Diabolus back toward the glass room.

Church grinned. "Well done Pinks," he said watching the pair moving toward the room. Although his excitement was short-lived as Pinky screamed as her hand glowed red and she pulled it from the now laughing Diabolus.

"I will deal with you later," he snarled at Pinky and went back over to Church.

"Now Potts..." he stopped mid-sentence, snarled, and flew back to the glass room.

Church looked around at the Portal and breathed a sigh of relief.

Now filled with shimmering Rainbow and Crimson orbs that flew out towards the glass room, the cellar buzzed and crackled with energy. Keepers and Guides surrounded the room and Pinky gasped.

"I can see the Spirits," she said looking wide-eyed at the myriad of lights filling the cellar. "Wow, it's amazing."

"Pinky, put the three amulets on Ryan," said Granny Pearl as Spirit Keepers flew into Ryan's body.

Pinky placed the amulets on Ryan's chest and his body juddered.

"Sorry we took so long Church, but we needed to rejuvenate to have enough power to contain the Diabolus's," said Granny Pearl.

"What's happening?" gasped Pinky several minutes later as a cobalt blue mist oozed from Ryan's mouth and nose and then a dim blue light took human shape before Spirit Keepers and Guides large orbs surrounded it.

With Pinky's mouth agape, she saw the circle of Spirit Keepers and Guides moving towards the Portal with Eric's Diabolus drifting at its centre, trying in vain to barge its way out.

The lights went into the Portal and vanished.

"They're taking the weakened Diabolus to the afterlife to find peace," said Granny Pearl.

"What's happening? I'm bloody starving," said a croaky voice behind them.

"Ryan, you dopey twonk," yelled Pinky turning around and saw Ryan sat up looking dazed. With a smile a mile wide, she went over, knelt beside him, and pecked him on his cheek.

"Urgh, get off... what's happening?

Pinky smiled and picked the amulets off the floor beside him. "Here, hold these," she said.

Ryan looked confused but clutched the amulets and his jaw dropped. "Whoa, what are they?"

"They are Keepers and Guides Ryan," said Granny Pearl.

"Granny Pearl!" exclaimed Ryan sounding surprised with his

eyebrows raised. He then smirked, "so that's what you look like.

Granny Pearl chuckled as Ryan looked over at the glass room. "I see you got old Adolf trapped but where's the other bugger? And what are those two in the coffin? "

"That is my wife and son," said Twigg hovering beside them, "I need to rescue them but with the demonic symbols on the walls, no Spirits can enter the glass room.

"And they've taken the other evil sod to the afterlife," said Pinky looking relieved.

"What are you thinking Church?" asked Granny Pearl picking up his emotion of intrigue.

Church puckered his brow and said. "Gran, if the symbols on the walls are to keep Spirits out, and the ones on the coffin are to keep them in... how about we do a little exchange?"

They listened while Church outlined his plan.

Granny Pearl's Spirit sounded worried. "It's risky Church; you know we can't enter the room to protect you should you fail."

Church nodded. "I know Gran, but as long as I take enough reinforcements with me, we should be okay."

"Are you feeling up to it Ryan?" asked Church, realising he must be exhausted after his battle.

Ryan shrugged. "Apart from being hungry, I feel great. I don't know what happened but I want to kick that evil Krauts arse."

"Right team, I will hold the amulets while you hold on to me; we will then have the amplified power of three," said Church.

The three tentatively walked through the door of the glass room surrounded by shimmering lights of the multi-coloured Spirits outside, and watched by the Diabolus within, awaiting its opportunity.

With Pinky and Ryan's hand on Church's shoulder, the three

shuffled over to the crystal coffin where Freda and Ulrich's Crimson auras now spun wildly.

The Diabolus snarled and spat fury as he rushed towards them and then backed away.

With one hand on Church's shoulder, Ryan and Pinky opened the glass lid.

"Thank you," said Freda, and Church felt the relief from her and Ulrich before their Spirits shot out of the room. The three smiled as they saw them reunited with Twigg outside as the Diabolus snarled and then gave a throaty laugh.

"So Potts, you have released my prisoners. You achieved nothing, they were of no further use to me... but you are."

The Diabolus's black aura crackled and expanded, surrounding the team as the amulets glowed and, combined with their gifted powers, formed a glowing bubble of energy around them.

Tingles of electricity coursed through them all, and with the heat now given off by the amulets, Church's hands felt on fire.

Like a misty black sponge, the Diabolus's power drained their protective bubble, and they all screamed with pain as the Diabolus released jolts of its demonic power.

With concerned Spirit Keepers and Guides yelling outside, the Diabolus overpowered the three and their energy bubble collapsed, sending them sprawling to the floor.

Although the struggle had weakened the Diabolus, it knew that once it had its vessel, it would be unstoppable.

Pinky and Ryan gasped and looked terrified as they saw the Diabolus entering Church, sniggering.

Ryan and Pinky saw Church's body jerking and looked at each other. "It is in for a shock, but I hope Church knows what he's doing," said Ryan with a quiver in his voice.

Pinky sighed and nodded. The pair then picked up Church and

placed him into the crystal coffin, with Freda and Ulrich's old skeletons crumbling under his weight.

"Surprise!" exclaimed Granny Pearl's Rainbow orb as the Diabolus large black orb appeared within Church's inner being.

The weakened Diabolus felt stunned as Rainbow orbs surrounded it. Like a pack of dogs on a fox, they harassed the demon draining his power further with every assault. Overwhelmed, it fought Spirit Keepers, sending some fleeing after almost draining their power, but each assault weakened the Diabolus further.

"I hope there are enough of us, we can't get any more reinforcements into the room without you bringing them in Church, and this Diabolus is powerful," said Granny Pearl and Church felt her concern.

"I know Gran, but if I bought any more of you, it would have noticed. I just hope we're weakening it enough," said Church as he watched his Trojan Horse army of Spirits dwindling and as the Diabolus raged, he and Granny Pearl joined the fray.

Pinky and Ryan became concerned when they saw Rainbow orbs shooting from Church, but they could only watch helplessly as Church's body convulsed for thirty-minutes before going still.

Pinky and Ryan then saw black mist oozing from Church's mouth and nose as more Rainbow orbs shot from his body.

The symbols on the glass walls then glowed red before disappearing and the Keeper's and Guide's outside hovered in and surrounded the coffin.

"What happened?" asked Ryan with his mouth agape.

"They've beaten it," said a Spirit Keeper sounding relieved.

"Now!" yelled Granny Pearl as her orb left Church's body.

Ryan and Pinky heaved Church from the coffin through the

black mist, laid him on the floor, closed the lid, and placed the three amulets on top.

Church opened his eyes and breathed a sigh of relief as he looked up at the black mist swirling inside its glass prison.

"Are you okay Grandson?" asked Granny Pearl as her orb formed to human shape.

Church nodded. "Yes, I'm fine Gran. Do you think that will contain it? It appeared to be getting its power back quickly," said Church as the black mist became more intense.

"I hope so, we need to keep it contained here, solid objects can't travel to the Spirit World, and we can't risk it getting loose. Unlike the other one, we can't defeat this Demon, it is far too powerful. It would wreak havoc in the Spirit World should we try to take it through to the afterlife."

"So what are we going to do with it?" asked Ryan as the coffin filled with an agitated black swirling mist. "It doesn't look like it can escape."

Granny Pearl sighed. "I don't know Ryan. It will be safe here for now, and with no surviving Hansens, their Portal will be closed, so it can't go anywhere."

"The problem will be that it will find a way out, even if it takes generations, someone would find it and not knowing what it was open the coffin," said Church frowning. He then juddered, "it will then have a host."

He could feel his Grandmother's energy waning as Grandpa Jack, also sounding drained, said. "We can deal with that later Church, we need to rejuvenate."

Church nodded and an exodus of Rainbow and Crimson Spirits headed into the Hansens Portal and vanished.

Church, Pinky, and Ryan looked at the floor of the Portal as it glowed bright white for an instant and then appeared again as an old wooden cellar floor.

"Well, that's the Portal closed," said Church and pointed to the coffin and the slow swirling black mist within, "and old buggerlugs must have realised he can't get out."

Ryan walked over to the rectangular red chest and picked it up. "Huh, it isn't heavy," he said and shook it, "and there doesn't seem to be a lot in here, I wonder what all the fuss was about? What does Buch Mose mean Church?" He asked, reading the thick black letters stencilled across the top.

"It means Genesis Ryan, and we can find out more once we get rid of the pair upstairs."

8

Obstacles do not exist to be surrendered to, but only to be broken

The four-wheel-drive SUV bumped along the small track through the fresh alpine Black Forest. Its two occupants felt ecstatic as they grinned at one another after following Church's order, as their handler had told them too. "I am happy he ordered us to go home, Olaf," said Hilda, pecking him on the cheek.

"Hmm umm, this ham hock's delicious," mumbled Ryan with his mouth full. He waved the gnawed hock at Church and Pinky. "Sure you don't want some?"

Church shook his head as he prized the old padlock off the Genesis chest with a crowbar and lifted the lid, while Pinky put another log on the fire as they sat in the kitchen of the Hansen's quaint country cottage.

Church peered into the Genesis chest. He took out two thick buff folders, two journals, and a magazine and placed them on the kitchen table.

"It's all in German," mumbled Ryan waving the hock bone

at the pile. "What does 'Tag des jüngsten Gerichts, Ende der Welt,' mean?" he asked, glancing at the front cover of the larger journal.

"It means Doomsday Ryan," said Church, picking up one folder with Josef Mengele written on the front that piqued his interest. He looked inside and took out the documents.

Pinky opened another folder, but when she saw gruesome photographs inside, her eyes widened. She gasped, clasped a hand over her mouth, and closed the folder.

Ryan wiped his greasy hands on his jeans before picking up a glossy magazine with 'Colonia Dignidad' written along the top and flicked through it.

Church looked up and said. "Schroder, that name sounds familiar." He stared at a photograph taken years earlier of Paul Schroder and looked at the cellar door and frowned, "and his face reminded me of someone."

"Paul Schroder, yeah, he was on the news on TV before we left England," said Pinky.

Church handed her the photo and she nodded. "Yep, that's him; he looked younger there, but he's that retired American Secret Service Director who was with the former US President when he died."

Church read out other documents in the folder about Wilhelm and Jessica Heinsling, describing them and their whereabouts until 1960. The document stated that the Heinsling's were staunch Nazis. Willhelm was a Nazi spy who worked as an intelligence officer during the war for the US government. Although spending most of his time in the States, he had returned to Germany toward the end of the war after his cover was almost blown. Jessica gave birth to their son a year after they returned, and at the end of the war, they'd escaped through the German ratlines. They returned to America and adopted the name they went under during Wilhelm's espionage days, William and Claire Schroder and their son, Paul. With the family already known as US citizens, nobody suspected their double lives, and William got a job with US intelligence. The last report in 1960 was brief. It stated that William died, but his son Paul had a good position within the US Secret Service.

The three looked confused. "So Paul Schroder's Hitler's kid," said Ryan, "do you think that's who old buggerlugs wanted us to give something to?"

Pinky puckered her brow. "I don't understand why; he's retired. He won't have any clout, especially with his old boss now dead."

Church furrowed his brow, shrugged, and picked up another folder while Ryan continued reading the magazine. "I wonder why this magazine is in there? I wonder where it is? It looks like an Amish Community somewhere, but it's all written in German," said Ryan.

Church sat back and gasped.

With a look of fear in his eyes, he told them. "I don't think Schroder was the son Hitler wanted to give something to, and he is a lot older now." He then showed the pair most recent photograph of a man.

Ryan furrowed his brow, "It's another one of Schrod... oh," he gasped as he looked closer. "It's not Schroder."

Church shook his head and read more papers from the folder.

He then waved the pages in his hand. "This is the connection that we have been looking for," he said and showed them the file of Martina and Stefan Goetz, who became Joseph and Jane Wolffe and their son, George.

Church read aloud information from the documents about the

Wolffe's. "It said that Joseph was one of the top German Rocket scientists who America brought to the US with his wife and baby son after the war under Operation Paperclip. Apart from a copy of their new US identity papers and their sons US birth certificate, it doesn't give a lot of information about Joseph's work in the US or his son, but... oh, hang on what do we have here."

Church took out another A4 sized sheet that looked written more recently by hand and his eyebrows rose as he read the writers name.

"Hitler wrote this," said Church as he read out the top of the document written in felt pen. 'Unser auserwählter Sohn,' Our chosen son.

"The papers were details about George Wolffe, who, Hitler had learned from television in the seventies, was becoming a powerful political figure in the United States." Church read on. "It said here that his son later became heavily involved with Ronald Reagan's Star Wars project." Church looked up and pointed to the photograph. "That's when that photograph must have been taken."

Church looked at the document and continued. "Hitler then wrote: My son wants to create weapons giving him absolute power. There is no doubt in my mind this is the son who emulated me. With my help, he will become the leader of the country that became my enemy. Father and son will then unleash Armageddon and annihilate the unworthy. Our new Reich will then rule our world."

"Unworthy, that sounded like anyone who wasn't a Nazi," said Pinky who shuddered.

Pinky, Ryan and Church looked at one another and then Church picked up the smaller of the two journals.

He opened the journal with Die Endlösung, The Final Solution, on the front.

Flicking through the first pages that appeared to be ramblings and ink drawings, he looked at the back and read several pages before looking at Pinky and Ryan who looked intrigued.

"This must be Hitler's journal from when he was alive," he said and flicked to the last few pages. "Huh, it's not dated but these last entries are in the same handwriting as the sheet about his son and written in felt pen," Church then sounded wistful. "It must be as we thought, he only died around forty-years ago."

He looked at the journal and said, "It looked like everything had been set in motion for Hitler's resurrection on a specific date."

Pinky and Ryan looked taken aback. "What makes you think that Church?" asked Pinky.

"Well," said Church, "Hitler wrote a passage from the bible, GENESIS 121: The LORD had said to Abraham, Go from your country, your people, and your father's household to the land I will show you."

"What's the significance? Hitler was a demon, not a religious nut."

Church shook his head and said, "Yes Ryan, but the things I read about Hitler during this investigation, he seemed to believe that supernatural forces protected him and was always spouting off passages from the bible in his speeches. Hitler wanted the German people to believe he was a messenger sent by God."

Church tapped on the journal and said. "Looking at some sketches at the start of the journal, it appeared Hitler wanted his followers around the world to build temples and monuments to worship him." Church rubbed his chin. "Today is April 22nd; the Diabolus came to our portal two days ago on the 20th of April."

"So?"

"So Pinky, that would have been Hitler's 121st birthday, the same as the psalm number, so the date of his encounter was not coincidental, he planned it years ago.

"So, the former US Presidents death may not have been from natural causes."

"Hmm, maybe not Ryan, it now looks unlikely," said Church.

"Do you think his son is also a Diabolus?"

Church looked pensive as he rubbed his chin and shrugged, "I don't know Pinky, perhaps. I never saw a black aura around him on TV, but cameras don't show aura's."

Ryan scratched his chin. "I wouldn't think it mattered to his nibs downstairs. His son is already old, but he has kids and grandkids the Diabolus could groom."

Church nodded, looked at Pinky, and smirked. "Or, Hitler could have more children in new bodies. The Diabolus could change bodies whenever it felt like it."

Pinky cringed as Church smirked and said. "Don't worry Pinks; he won't be spreading his seed again anytime soon."

Pinky shuddered and squinted. "Bloody good job... creepy git."

"So, what do you think Hitler wanted to give his war-monger son?"

Church picked up the doomsday journal of loose handwritten sections and seeing some pages faded knew it had been written over several years. He looked at the handwriting, so knew it was by the same individual and said. "This must be what he wanted his son to have, Ryan."

"What is it?"

"I'm not sure Pinky," said Church flicking through the pages, "but it was written by Adolf Eichmann, the Nazi responsible for many atrocities during WW2 with chemical weapons. He escaped after the war and I think I read about them finding and executing him in the 1960s."

Church furrowed his brow as he read more of the journal. "I don't understand any of this. The first document is dated 1944 and looked to be chemical formulas and weird scientific jargon. It looked like they carried on with experiments after the war because the last entry is dated 1958, and are more chemical formulas and equations. It must be some kind of destructive weapon that Hitler wanted he, and his son, to unleash onto the world."

Pinky picked up the folder that had shocked her and showed them the photographs of piled bodies, with close-up images of distorted faces that looked like they died in agony.

Church cringed as he read the German writing on the top of one photograph of a large pile of distorted Chinese corpses. He looked at Pinky and Ryan and gasped. "It said this was the result from 0.01mmol/L of the doomsday formula."

The three looked at one another. "Armageddon," said Church, "that's what he wanted to give his son."

Pinky looked confused. "But there must be a cure. Why would his son destroy the human race and himself along with it?"

"That's probably in here Pinky, but we don't need to look any further," said Church glancing at the logs ablaze in the fireplace. "There's only one place this belongs. Grab everything, we will burn it all."

Ryan and Pinky nodded, took the paperwork from the table, and walked over to the fire.

"No, Church, Stop!" yelled a familiar voice behind them.

9

It is not the truth that matters, but victory

"I have a bad feeling about this Church," said Ryan with a quake in his voice.

Pinky nodded and held up the Washington Post newspaper. "Me too, especially after reading how Paul Schroder was found dead in police cells after being arrested in connection with the assassination of former President Grahame. It said the CIA discovered Schroder used their covert drug to cause the President's heart attack. Perhaps someone used the same drug to kill him."

Church nodded feeling perplexed. "It makes no sense, it didn't say who killed him, and I don't understand why," he furrowed his brow, "unless they didn't know."

"Or his brother had him bumped off to stop him blabbering, they both sound like evil bastards," said Ryan and took a deep breath, "it looks like we are going from one wolf's lair into another."

"Yeah, but this one is the most powerful wolf on the planet," said Pinky.

Church nodded, looked sullen, and although felt terrified, said. "Granny Pearl wouldn't put us in harm's way and the Spirit World must have their reasons."

"Ladies and Gentleman, we are about to land at Ronald Reagan International Airport, please fasten your safety..."

"Be careful what you say team," said Church over the announcement. "This man is dangerous."

* * *

"Here George," said his wife Anne, handing him a glass of freshly squeezed orange juice.

"Who was that on the phone?" she asked, as she sat next to him on the plush sofa.

George sighed, and in his articulate American accent said. "Senator John McMahon; he told me not to worry, they were whipping up a media storm so everything should soon be over. They will make it appear as if they forced me out of office."

George took a sip of the tangy juice, looked concerned, and said. "I am not up to this job honey. I am a scientist, not a politician, I hope the Senate can sort this out quickly and I can get back to work as normal."

Anne chuckled and swept back his grey hair over his ear. "Your normal and everyone else's normal was entirely different, Wolffe." She leant over and pecked her husband on the cheek. "Have you made any progress with the antidote?"

George sighed, shook his head, and looked into his elegant seventy-year-old wife's comforting brown eyes. "No, we know nothing about the weapon, so we can't produce a countermeasure."

"Oh, Sarah called and said our guests have arrived and she's on her way," said Anne and smiled.

George pierced his lips and puckered his brow. "Great honey, I hope they have the answers we need."

Anne looked into her husband's weary old eyes and saw fear and concern. She also felt scared but didn't want to show it and asked. "Did they uncover anything from Paul Schroder's autopsy?"

George shook his head. "No, whatever they used to assassinate Paul coagulated his blood, so if they gave him the antidote, we couldn't have found it."

Anne looked shocked. "You and Paul were friends; I wonder why he killed Bill Grahame?"

George furrowed his brow and shook his head. "I don't know honey, I am shocked. I have known Paul since childhood. Our families came here from Germany after the war. People thought we were brothers as we looked so much alike."

"Maybe," said Anne and chuckled, "but you became far more successful... and handsome."

George smirked and kissed his wife, although Anne knew he felt troubled and foolish having not realised that his childhood buddy and murderer of his friend President Bill Grahame, was a member of the powerful, secretive, modern-day Nazis.

George heaved a sigh and rubbed his temples. "I don't know what to do. This has all happened so fast, and it's down to me to find a solution."

"I am sure you will George, you are a genius, and thanks to the CIA uncovering Paul's connection with that Nazi sect they have been investigating, you now know about the weapon and can stop it."

"I hope so honey," said George and smiled, trying to hide his uncertainty and reassure his wife.

George felt terrified. He and the US intelligence teams knew nothing about the weapon, apart from it being a bio-plague that once released would unleash a catastrophic event onto the unsuspecting world.

George's phone rang and the image of a stern-faced man appeared on the screen.

"Hi Chuck, any more news?" asked George with a quiver in his voice.

The man on screen, looking dismayed and sounding angry, said. "Yes Mr President, our agent within the colony got news to our contact in Santiago earlier. He said they suspected him of being a spy and he feared for his life. Our contact said the communication between the pair suddenly ended and he heard gunfire, so he is probably dead."

George sighed and looked sullen, "I am sorry to hear that Chuck," he said, surprised by the man's blasé tone.

Chuck cleared his throat and said. "He told our agent before he died that the upper echelons of the colony have been telling their followers to prepare." The man glared at George, his cold eyes made him feel uneasy as he told him, "our spy overheard phone conversations between the leader of Colonia Dignidad and what he assumed were other Nazi colonies around the world. He instructed them to ensure all their people were immunised as they expected the order to launch to come through at any time."

"Damn," said George trembling as he looked at the man glaring back at him. "Chuck, we don't yet have any defence. Have you any idea who will give that order? Maybe we can find and stop him.

The CIA Director glowered at George and with contempt in

his voice said. "Yes sir, they are awaiting your order... Mr President."

George still felt shaken as his wife and Sarah, the Wolffe family's special friend, sat in the lounge next to the Oval Office comforting him. "I don't understand," he said taking a sip of Brandy, "Who do the Nazi's think I am? Why are they waiting for me to give the order to destroy the world?"

"I don't know honey," said Anne, "perhaps they believed the rumours that the Senate spread years ago about you being a war-monger who had journalists murdered."

"Perhaps Honey, but they did that for good reason," said George and sighed. "I am a rocket scientist like my father. I only went into politics to further our research and the Senate and Bill Graham only made me Vice President so I could convince other world leaders to get their top scientists and engineers involved with the Ark project."

"We know that honey, but nobody else does."

Sarah shuddered, looked behind George and Anne, and smiled.

"Are you okay Sarah? You look like you have seen a ghost."

Sarah chuckled. "I'm fine Anne." She leant over, held George's hand, and whispered. "George, I think you may soon have your answers."

The intercom buzzed and the President's head of security announced. "Mr President, your guests have arrived."

Church, Ryan, and Pinky gasped when they entered the room.

Along with President George Wolffe, the first lady, and Sarah a mortal Spirit Guide; Pinky and Ryan smelt peppermint coming from the shimmering Crimson Spirit stood in the corner of the room, who said. "Hi team; I'm Joanie, Sarah's Spirit Guide. I will come back later because my temporary Portal is draining me. You need to show George what you have and perhaps together you can come up with a solution to avoid Armageddon."

Joanie vanished as George, unaware of Joanie's presence, went over, and extended his hand. "Hi team, I'm George."

George took them over, introduced Anne, and then smirked when he introduced Sarah.

"She's one of yours," he chuckled, "would you like some tea?"

With the power of the amulets worn off Ryan and Pinky, only Church could see Sarah's Crimson aura as the team shook hers and the first lady's hand.

"That's what old Adolf must have looked like in his old age, and without a hairy leach," whispered Ryan as the seventy-two-year-old President went and ordered them a pot of tea as they sat on the sofa around a coffee table.

Anne and Sarah chatted with the team until George came over and sat with his wife and Sarah.

"Well, he isn't a Diabolus," whispered Church, "his aura is white, the same as everyone's without the gift, so, unlike ours, it doesn't look like the demon gene was passed down."

"Yeah," said Pinky, "but he's still the son of Adolf Hitler... and a murderer."

George leant over and smiled. "I imagine you have a lot of questions about me?" he said in a soft tone that surprised the team.

'He doesn't sound like Hitler,' thought Church, recalling the black and white newsreels of the dictator spouting his doctrine to the German masses. He nodded and said. "Yes, we do, Mr President."

The President smiled. "Please, call me George. I understand your concerns, but I will explain later as we have an urgent matter that I was told you can help with."

"How can we trust you when you have journalists and your

brother murdered," blurted Ryan.

George, Anne, and Sarah looked puzzled as Church threw Ryan a curt glare.

"The rumours about murdered journalist were nonsense. The evidence released was fake, contrived to scare the press and allow my husband to do his work. George has murdered no one and he doesn't have a brother," said Anne sounding angry.

Ryan looked sheepish as George, still looking confused about his outburst, tried to reassure the team. "The rumours were circulated by the Senate years ago so I could continue with my project unhindered. I will explain later but we need to deal with our major concern that affects the human race. I believe you have something vital that can help."

The team looked concerned at one another and George saw apprehension on their faces.

They then heard the Presidents voice trembling and saw the fear in his eyes when he said. "Please, you must trust me."

With his thoughts conflicted over whether this man was good or evil, George's calm tone and friendly demeanour eased Church's doubts. He rubbed his chin and thought. 'He could have had us killed on arrival by the Secret Service agents who met us at the airport. They could have just taken what he needed. Besides, Granny Pearl told us to trust him.'

Church nodded and took out the Doomsday journal, along with several folders Granny Pearl had instructed him to bring from his briefcase. He placed them on the table and George explained the planets quandary and then said. "All we know is that the missiles carrying the bioweapon are ready to launch; we also know it is a devastating airborne spread bio-plague that they intend to release into the Earth's atmosphere. The plague would cover the planet on the winds, so even if we destroy their facility, we cannot contain the plague.”

George looked at the team and sounding concerned told them. “Unless we have a countermeasure and I believe there must be an antidote for the plague so the Nazis can survive and take over the planet. If we could find that, we could produce a countermeasure and soak the area before we destroyed their underground facility before they launch their missiles.”

Pinky shuddered as she recalled the gruesome photographs from the folder she’d seen.

“I need to know what information you have that may help. Sarah seemed convinced that you have the answer,” said George rubbing his chin.

Recalling something George had told them, Ryan puckered his brow looking bemused. “You said they were ready to launch George, so why haven’t they?”

George, looking anxious and with a quake in his voice, told them what the CIA Director had said on the phone. He then looked perturbed and said. “Although I can’t understand why, at least if they are waiting for me to contact them it gives us time to come up with something.”

Looking frustrated, George threw out his hands in desperation and said. “I understand none of this... why me?”

Church leant back in the chair, rubbed his chin, looked at the distraught President, and handing him a folder, said. “Perhaps this will explain George. Do you want me to translate it for you?”

George, looking tentative, took the folder, read the front, and said, “Thanks Church but that won’t be necessary, my parents taught me German.”

Church saw sorrow in George’s eyes as he said. “My parents often spoke about Germany,” he sighed, “but memories of the horrors they had witnessed with its destruction during the

Second World War haunted them, so they never returned.

George cleared his throat, composed himself, and read the contents of the folder.

Church looked at Pinky and Ryan as they waited for George's reaction.

They saw Georges mouth agape as he read the documents about how Dr Joseph Mengele had inseminated five selected German women with Eva Braun's eggs, fertilised by Hitler's' sperm. He recalled how his mother had told him how she fell pregnant shortly after having her appendix removed. Something else his parents had told him now concerned him as he read more documents.

George's voice trembled and he gasped. "Paul Schroder was my brother."

He looked up at Ryan. "Now I understand what you meant before. But I assure you I had nothing to do with his murder... but we suspect who did, to stop him giving us details about his Nazi network."

George then looked sad and sounding hoarse, said. "My parents called me the miracle baby because they had been told they couldn't have children. They said the toxic chemicals used by my father in his work had made him infertile." He wiped a tear from his eye and said. "They never knew."

Church shook his head. "No George, I don't think any of them knew. IVF didn't exist in the forties, so someone must have developed it in secret. We found five folders, but three were marked deceased and with no information other than a sheet with details of the birth, we assumed they were killed during, or just after the war."

"It looked like only you and Paul Schroder survived. Hitler wanted his new Reich to take over the planet, with your help.

He knew you were involved with Darth Reagan and his space blasters," said Ryan still unsure about the President.

George sat back and looked confused at the three. "But I don't understand; Hitler died over seventy-years-ago."

Church looked at Pinky and Ryan and leant forward. "Did Sarah tell you anything about us?

George nodded. "Yes, a little. I know you are like her, powerful psychics who communicate with Spirits and may have the answers I need."

"That is all you need to know for now George. I will explain the rest later, but now we must focus on the bio-plague problem."

George nodded and took a deep breath. "Yes, you're right Church. What information do you have about it?"

Church handed George the doomsday journal.

The team saw the President's facial expressions changing as he read the scientific jargon and formulas.

He then looked up at the intrigued team and grinned. "Everything we need is in here Church." He tapped on a section. "Here is the antidote and our countermeasure."

Church looked at the relief on the President's face and asked. "That's great George, how long will it take you to make a countermeasure?"

George again looked at the formulas, smirked, and said. "We already have the main ingredients in the U.S. and vast quantities of it; we just need to add one more enzyme which looks simple to produce. I will call Professor Kyoto and he can make the enzyme."

George called the Professor who sounded delighted as George showed him the formula. "I can have the enzyme additive ready in a few hours George, it's simple to make, and we only need a small quantity to add to the main composite."

A steward came into the room with a fresh pot of tea and while Anne, Sarah, and the team sat chatting, George made phone calls to other world leaders and his war cabinet to convene a meeting for a few hours hence in the Oval Office.

Anne and Sarah looked confused as they overheard George instructing the US Air Commodore to arrange with the campus in Atlanta for several tankers of their product.

With George preoccupied, Anne showed the PATH team to the White House guest quarters and then went back to the living room to watch TV and wait for George to finish his briefing.

While Ryan demolished several steaks in the dining room, Church and Pinky spoke with Sarah and a rejuvenated Joanie.

"It's strange how a Spirit Guide is friends with the American President. How did you meet George, Sarah?"

Sarah smirked. "We have been friends for many years. His father Joseph contacted Joanie when he passed over and requested I found an important item and give it to his son. I felt shocked when I learned that George was at the time the Governor of California, and even more surprised when the item turned out to be a tatty old pocket watch of no monetary value.

Sarah took a sip of lemon tea and in her southern American drawl, continued. "Anyhow, it turned out the pocket watch was only a ruse. Joseph knew his analytical and curious son would want to know more about me and how I came across it, but I wouldn't tell him at first."

"Gangsters hunted Sarah after she returned the gold and paperwork from a deceased mob boss to his son. They thought she was part of a rival criminal network," said Joanie, "she needed help and turned to George."

Sarah nodded and said. "George used his power and influence to have the gangsters caught."

Sarah looked appreciative as she recalled the events and told them. "George asked nothing in return for his help, so I knew this was a man who we could trust. With the Spirit Worlds blessing, I told him a little about who I was, and what I do," she beamed, "that was many years ago and we have been great friends ever since."

The PATH team looked at the middle-aged Guide with auburn hair and rosy cheeks and smiled.

10

Strength lies not in defence but in attack

With Breakfast over, the adults and children went to the centre of the village.

They gathered around a cenotaph containing the ashes of their dead founder and his wife.

A smiling elderly man sat in his wheelchair in front of a smooth white marble statue on the cenotaph.

After giving a short rousing speech, he went silent.

The people smiled up at the statue of a stern-faced man holding a book in one hand and a gun in the other, with a marble hairy leach under his nose.

They snapped to attention and saluted the statue.

Morning worship over, the children went to their classrooms while the farmers went to the fields.

A uniformed man wheeled the old man to a brick building followed by men and women, either dressed in old military uniform or blue coveralls.

A group of officers went into the building while others waited outside for the elevators return.

The adults of Colonia Dignidad went about their tasks within the large colony above and below ground.

The surface colony looked like a small village with wood and brick houses surrounded by acres of fields and orchards.

With farmers dressed in simple homemade clothing and the men sprouting long beards, it resembled an Amish community.

Brick buildings were at the centre of the colony. These were the school, shops, clinic, community centre, dining rooms, and an old brick room with four elevators.

Above ground, the colony, surrounded by fields of cereals and root vegetables, had meadows with livestock grazing and poultry pens, with the animals providing meat and dairy products for the colony.

With acres of fruit trees in bloom, the smell of blossom drifted on the light breeze. The colonists' looked forward to their annual crop of pears that they knew would come soon in this temperate climate. They all worked hard and enjoyed the simple lifestyle in their self-sufficient community.

Several tractors ploughed the soil on fallow fields to prepare them for sowing. They heard faint rumblings in the sky above them and looked up.

"Those rain clouds look strange," said one tractor driver, wiping sweat from his brow as all workers in the fields gazed at the dark clouds descending above their heads.

"Good, it will refresh the air," said his wife as she jumped off the tractor and removed her bonnet to let the rain fall onto her head. "I've never seen rain like this before," she said as droplets fell onto her skin.

Everyone looked at each other confused as the clouds neared

the ground.

"This rain smells strange," said a farmer and licked his skin.

The black clouds hit the colonists, drenching them and the surrounding land of the colony.

The colonist's, now soaked and feeling confused, looked at one another.

"It tastes like Coca-Cola," said a farmer looking bemused.

"All six have flown over, sir," said the officer looking at the screen. "They did not deviate from their course or altitude."

The Major looked at the computer screen and read the information: Kc10 Extender Refuelling Tankers - no weaponry.

"Very well, there's nothing to worry about," said the Major.

The underground bunker beneath the colony was immense. Its huge laboratories contained flasks of the biogenic plague. It also housed numerous ICBM's in silos, packed with enough explosives to ensure maximum coverage of their deadly payloads into Earth's atmosphere. With high-tech missiles, worldwide targeting and surveillance equipment, it was an impenetrable fortress.

Unlike the concrete and metal bunkers of the 1940s, this one was reinforced with layers of tungsten and titanium interwoven strands. With the layers compressed, it spread any impact and could withstand most weapons.

Along with the military personnel and scientists, the new world order of Nazi leaders also stayed inside the bunker, coordinating the worldwide Nazi network.

Everyone inside the bunker now felt a buzz of excitement, knowing the time was close.

Karl Schafer sat in his wheelchair in the large conference room surrounded by various military officers dressed in different

German uniforms of the Second World War.

From the Wehrmacht to the SS, they sat around a conference table as screens around the room showed faces of other Nazi party leaders around the world dressed in similar attire.

They all looked at their elderly leader, Karl, who had a fire in his eyes as he sat back in his wheelchair and smiled.

"Not long now," he said, "according to the instructions our Führer gave me before he died, he will now be resurrected and in a vessel, bringing his son."

Everyone in the room, along with those on the screens, smiled, and with a hitlergruss, shouted. "Heil Hitler!"

"Is everything prepared? We have a long task ahead rebuilding the Reich," said Schafer, looking at the faces on the screens around the room.

"We are all immunised," said the French Nazi delegate, followed by the other 46 delegates, echoing the same confirmation.

"And Schroder... Did you deal with him?" asked Schafer, his voice sounding abrupt.

"Yes sir, but he was a loyal Nazi," said the US delegate looking angry.

"He knew the risks," said Schafer and frowned.

He sat back in his wheelchair, looked at everyone in the room and on the screen.

Smirking, he announced, "Excellent... Ladies and Gentlemen, let us await our Führer and his son, the US President... and prepare for our new world."

The satellite radar stations lit up. "Sir, we have multiple inbound targets," shouted an officer in SS uniform sounding anxious and looking horrified.

The Major went over and looked at a computer screen. He

took a sharp intake of breath and his eyes widened as he saw the numbers, type, and armament of inbound aircraft and incoming ICBM's on the computer screen. "The sky's full of them," he gasped, "how long before they reach here, Lieutenant?"

"About fifteen minutes, sir."

"Prepare defensive measures," ordered the Major, and trembling, he picked up a red telephone.

The control centre was a flurry of activity as personnel scrambled to activate the missile and artillery defence systems.

After the Major finished his conversation with Schafer and hung up, the people in the control centre went silent, awaiting his next order. The Major looked over to one consul and the Captain at the station clicked his heels together. With sharpness in his voice, the Major then ordered.

"Launch the weapon!"

While the Captain entered the launch sequence into the computer and the control centre personnel sat silently at their posts staring at weapons systems screens; the Major looked up at the ceiling and thought. 'God help us all.'

11

Success is the sole earthly judge of right and wrong

"The world owes you a tremendous debt of gratitude team," said George walking into the living room after leaving the Oval Office.

He sat with them around the coffee table and a steward poured the tired President a mug of coffee and left the room.

"Did everything go okay, George?" asked Church, seeing the President looking fretful.

George nodded and looked at the PATH team, his wife, and Sarah.

He took a drink of coffee and told them. "Several aircraft were destroyed with their ground to air missiles."

He cupped his hands around the mug and said. "The pilots reported wiping out the surface colony within minutes but their weapons had no effect on the underground bunker."

Then George looked at the five and continued. "Until they

made the mistake of opening the silo doors to launch the ICBM's carrying the bio-weapon. Our bombs and missiles hit them and breached the bunker."

George leant back and with a quake in his voice said, "We have destroyed everything there."

The five heaved sighs of relief and Church noticed George looking glum as he told them.

"Our surveillance drones showed deep smouldering craters with a huge bunker with flames and black smoke billowing from the missile silos."

"How about the bio-weapons, did any launch?" asked Ryan leaning forward.

George shook his head. "No Ryan, none were launched because there was no bio-plague detected in the atmosphere by our converted AWAC's, thanks to your countermeasure." He then looked sullen and sighed. "Nobody could have survived that inferno."

They all thought the President would look more relieved as George took another drink of coffee and mumbled. "I sacrificed all those people and my job is to save lives," he grimaced, "this job sucks."

Anne knew how guilty and distraught her husband felt after having to decide something of that magnitude, and Church, seeing the remorse in the President's eyes, said. "You had no choice George and the people who died will now be at peace in the afterlife."

Anne leant across and whispered in George's ear, "I am proud of you honey. You did what was necessary to protect ours, and all people around the world's families."

George smiled, leant over, kissed his wife's forehead, and sat back and looked at the five.

"Troops and equipment from the aircraft carriers USS Gerald R. Ford and Admiral Kuznetsov are on the way to the site to help the Chileans with the clean-up operations. The Chilean government press agency will release news later of an asteroid strike on an uninhabited area of scrubland." George took another drink, "security agencies worldwide are searching for the rest of the Nazi underground network."

George then puckered his brow and looked at Church. "Now this is over Church, will you tell me more about who you are, and how you know so much about me and Adolf Hitler?"

Church looked taken aback and felt unsure what information he could divulge.

Sarah then smiled at him as the aroma of peppermint and brussels sprouts filled the room.

"You can tell George about the encounter with the Diabolus Church; he can help with our problem," said Granny Pearl.

George and Anne turned around as Church, Ryan, Sarah and Pinky looked over their shoulders at the Spirits behind them; but seeing, hearing, and smelling nothing, they turned back around. George smirked and said, "We have other guests I take it."

Church smiled, nodded, and after Granny Pearl and Joanie vanished, he related their story to George, Anne, and Sarah. He told them about the PATH team, their Portal, and their encounter with Hitler's Diabolus and its intention to use his and Ryan's body to contact George, and together unleash Armageddon. Pinky and Ryan quivered when Church recounted the epic battle with the Diabolus and how they and the Spirits had subdued it. He ended by telling George where they had the Diabolus contained and the problem they now faced.

George, knowing a little about the Spirit World from Sarah, didn't appear alarmed or surprised with Church's story, and once he'd finished, the smart analytic scientist said. "Joseph and Jane Wolffe were my parents, and although Paul Schroder was my childhood friend, he was not my brother," he smirked and said, "the fools killed him unaware he was also Hitler's son. Hitler chose the wrong sibling for his evil scheme."

The team saw sadness and pride in the President's eyes when he said. "Hitler was correct when he wrote that he thought I emulated him, my father. But he was not my father, Joseph Wolffe was." George smiled, "and not only was he a pioneering scientist and an engineering genius, but after witnessing the destruction and death caused by weapons he'd developed for Hitler during the war, he was a man dedicated to peace and helping humanity, as am I."

George sat back in the chair and with a glint in his eyes, smiled, and said. "I think I can solve your problem team. Please come with me, I want to show you something."

The PATH team looked confused as George took them down an elevator and into a large room beneath the White House.

"It looks like the pictures on TV of the NASA control centre," said Ryan as he looked at consuls manned by people wearing thin headsets giving instructions.

"It's similar Ryan," said George, and took them over to a large flat screen on the far wall.

"So, you brought us here to watch a Sci-Fi movie. Where has the Starship Enterprise gone? And what are those little dots of light flitting about that structure?" asked Pinky, puckering her brow and pointing at the screen.

George chuckled, "No Starship Enterprise I'm afraid, and this isn't a movie Pinky," he said and pointed at the screen, "That is a space dock under construction now in Earth's upper orbit."

The PATH team stood with mouths agape as George zoomed in

on what looked like the brightly lit skeleton of an aircraft hangar floating in space. "This is the Space Ark project my father and I conceived and designed decades ago," said George and smiled, "that's Ronald Reagans Star Wars programme."

The team looked taken aback as George told them. "Although the administrations that followed Ronald's tried to scrap the project, thanks to Bill Grahame, over the past few years I have been able to turn our dream into reality."

"Wow!" exclaimed Ryan as the images zoomed in further showing the dots to be astronauts in robotic suits working on the immense structure.

"That thing's huge George, what's it for?"

"It's a spaceport to assemble sections of the Space Arks when they have finished building them on Earth, Church."

The team looked puzzled. "What's a Space Ark George?" asked Church scratching his chin.

George smiled and took them into a suite at the back, poured them each a mug of coffee, and explained about the Space Arks.

The team looked enthralled as George told them about how he, along with the world's best scientists and engineers, were building immense spacecraft to transport people to other planets when they discovered one suitable and able to sustain human life.

"For the past few years, as Vice President, I have been persuading world leaders to become involved in the project instead of throwing their countries money and resources into nuclear weapons."

"But according to the news reports other countries around the world feared you because you've hated them for years."

George smirked, "Yes, that's true Pinky, but that is what ours and other world leaders spread around their countries media to stop them investigating. None of them wanted news about the project known until we were ready to let them know because it would jeopardise the project. Governments feared the consequences would be dire if their populations found out they were spending a fortune of their tax money and resources to help America with their crazy scheme."

"Hmm, I wondered why that chubby bloke with the daft haircut hadn't been on the news for years testing his nukes."

George chuckled. "I won't tell my friend Kim Jong-un what you called him the next time we speak Pinky."

"Getting other countries to stop their nuclear weapons programmes must have been a monumental task George."

George nodded, "You're right Church. The world feared us with our vast nuclear arsenal and strived to compete, although nobody understood why," said George and threw out his hands. "Why have the capability to destroy our planet many times over... it's crazy, and Bill Grahame and the other world leaders knew it. Even though in some countries people lived in poverty because of the cost of upgrading new weapons, they didn't want to stop, fearing they would be defenceless."

George leant forward, looked at the team, and said. "Although nobody outside the government and a few security agencies know; President Graham disarmed our nukes several years ago and other countries followed suit. They instead became involved with the Ark project." George sighed, "Bill was a great President committed to making the world safe... and a good friend. He, like me and the other leaders, also knew that with the current rate of growth, Earth could not sustain the human population of future generations. We needed to build new homes in space until we find a new planet to call home."

"But that could take generations to find a planet and then

get people to it George," said Church, finishing his coffee and looking intrigued, but feeling unconvinced.

George nodded. "Yes Church, we realise that, but by building the Arks using the technology we have now, we can develop and improve them as we advance our knowledge."

"So you are building dockyards but have no ships," said Ryan sniggering.

George smiled, finished his coffee, and said. "Come with me guys."

He took them along to a consul and sat around the controller, who pointed to a screen.

"That is the Chinese Ark in Mongolia," said the controller and gave instructions in Chinese through her headset.

The PATH team watched live video footage from within a large, brightly lit construction hanger in Mongolia.

The Chinese consul operator spoke to the Director of the Chinese Ark, who pressed a control directing the cameras around the vessel.

Thirty minutes later, the team looked awestruck after watching the cameras showing them around the craft.

Ryan's eyebrows rose and he spluttered. "That thing's huge George, it looks bigger than a modern shopping mall, with cinemas, games room, and loads of food halls," he tapped his lips together, smirked, and said, "what a place to live."

George nodded and smiled. "That is only one section Ryan. There will be ten sections to each Ark and we are building twenty Arks from different countries to begin with. Once completed, these Arks will have enough resources to be self-sustaining, with schools, hospitals, botanical gardens, and livestock. Many people can live on them in Earth's orbit for however long they wish until we find a suitable planet. They will all have the recently developed solar drive propulsion systems, which we can upgrade as our technical knowledge improved.”

“It’s fantastic George,” gasped Ryan. “So when are you going to let the world know about this?”

George looked at the team and smirked. “Soon...very soon.”

George then took them to another screen in the control centre showing another image in space. “This is what I wanted to show you.”

“What’s that? The other one’s baby brother,” Pinky chortled when she looked at a smaller space dock.

“Something like that,” said George and smiled as he zoomed in a drone camera onto two astronauts in robotic exoskeletons working on the outside of a space vessel.

“It doesn’t look very big George,” said Church furrowing his brow, “judging by the size of the astronauts, it looked the same size as a bus.”

“Yeah, it looks like a space rocket from the old Buck Rogers movies,” said Ryan with a cheeky grin.

Pinky pointed at the screen. “And it doesn’t have any windows, so how are people going to see out?”

George cocked his head to one side, looked at the screen, and chuckled. “I suppose you’re right Ryan, it does look like an old prop from a 70s sci-fi series, and it doesn’t need to be large or have windows.”

George pointed to the screen and announced.

“That team... will solve your problem.”

12

Epilogue

The solar drive spacecraft streaked through the dark vacuum of space at light speed.

This sleek, silver unmanned spacecraft controlled by computers and robots hurtled through the cosmos on the pre-programmed route of its fantastic voyage.

This ultra-high-tech space reconnaissance vehicle was the first and most vital stage in George Wolffe's Space Ark project to find a suitable planet. Its voyage could take either years or span lifetimes in the search for a new home for the expanding human race.

With a worldwide audience glued to their TV's, computer screens, and tablets; live pictures of the launch from the small space dock beamed around the world. Everyone saw the space rocket's engines glow bright white before the ship disappeared among the stars.

Three in particular enjoyed the spectacular event and sniggered while watching TV in their quaint stone cottage within a clearing in a forest on the Yorkshire Moors.

The only occupant in the spaceship swirled around its crystal sarcophagus in the pitch-blackness.

The demon of the twentieth century's most notorious despot was on its endless journey to discover a new home for the people it had tried so hard to destroy.

THE END

Don't cry because it's over; smile because it happened.

I hope you enjoyed Return of the Reich. Reviews are important to independent authors. If you would be kind enough to write a review on any online retailer's sites, I would be extremely grateful, and possibly share my chocolate with you... possibly.

In the unlikely event that you didn't enjoy this little gem, please write bad reviews under my pen name, Charles Dickens... he won't mind.

Chapter headings are quotes coined by Adolf Hitler from Mein kampf

About the Author

Robert A Webster is an exciting comedy fiction writer.

His unique brand of snarky humour and imaginative storytelling breathe vivid life into his work, which combines comical British characters with exotic Southeast Asian settings.

The result is "brilliant" and "unpredictable," as Dinorah Blackman of Readers' Favorite says; awarding his books 5-star ratings.

Originally from Cleethorpes, UK, and now living in Cambodia, he embodies both hearty wit and adventurous vigour, making his prose insanely memorable and incessantly enjoyable.

His first novel *Siam Storm* received rave reviews in southeast Asia, with the sequels, *Chalice,* and *Bimat,* similarly acclaimed. *Protector,* the fourth book of the *Siam Storm* **series**, continues the journey of the lovable scallywags who have a penchant for mischief. The books document high-octane escapades and colourful, fantastical narratives that don't stop.

His other hilarious novels include **Fossils** and **Spice** and his journey into the paranormal genre with the **PATH** series makes him an adaptable imaginative writer.

Along with his fiction novels, he has two non-fiction works.
   Diabetes type 2 –How to help you safely lower your blood sugar with the tree of life, which follows his and co-authors research into the Moringa Tree and it benefits for Diabetics.

Something to Read While Travelling-Thailand. A comprehensive travel companion to accompany travellers on their journey through, The Land of Smiles.

His latest work, **Ratchet, and Stench - Animal Sleuths** is a children's adventure. Although written with the same wit as imagination as his adult novels, so it is appealing enough for anyone to read and enjoy.

When he's not crafting unforgettable stories, Robert enjoys snorkelling, self-deprecating humour, and the warm climate of Cambodia.

Also by Robert A Webster

SIAM STORM – A THAILAND ADVENTURE

A stolen holy relic from a secluded Thai Buddhist Monastery sends a combatant monk on a quest to retrieve the sacred item. Three English lads who are having the holiday experience of a lifetime in Thailand, become inadvertently embroiled in the deadly pursuit.

Enjoy the first adventure of Nick, Spock and Stu as they assist in the recovery of the relic and the subsequent voyage of discovery.

CHALICE – SIAM STORM 2 – A CAMBODIAN ADVENTURE

The discovery of a mysterious corpse leaves law enforcement agencies baffled. This adventure sees the lads join forces with their new friend, the mad monk, Pon, as they once again attempt to recover a holy relic, which has this time been stolen for a completely new and sinister reason. The chase takes them into Cambodia, as they thwart plans that could affect the planet and change them into fruit based drinkers.

BIMAT – SIAM STORM 3 – A VIETNAMESE ADVENTURE

A kidnap and ransom demand lead our hapless heroes into a pursuit through Vietnam. They encounter an old foe, driven by obsession in his revenge driven quest. This time, they face many challenges in both their adventure and their personal circumstance and although they almost lose everything, they never lose hope.

TRILOGY

All three Southeast Asia adventures.

PROTECTOR – SIAM STORM 4 – THE FINAL ADVENTURE

The adventure continues in, Protector, the fourth book of the Siam Storm Series...

When descendants of Siddhartha Gautama arrive at the Royal Palace in Bangkok; Prime Master Pon assembles a team to discover who is responsible for the murder of the other descendants, along with their age-old protectors.

The fun begins when Spock and Stu join the team, and as usual, they find trouble. Even with Spock and Stu underfoot, the team uncovers evidence of a plot with worldwide implications.

Protector follows the hazardous journey through unfamiliar terrain as the team races the clock to stop further killings of their brethren, only to discover that things are not always as they seem.

SIAM STORM – THE SERIES

The complete four-part series

SPICE

Ben Bakewell is a master baker with a unique gift, making him the grand master of his culinary craft. More commonly known as 'Cake,' he meets up with Ravuth, a Cambodian man residing in England and who has spent the majority of his life trying to trace his long lost family.

Jed Culver is a disgraced D.E.A agent whose bitterness for his old employer and lust for revenge lead him along a deadly path, as he also pursues the plant, although for a far more sinister gain.

This thrilling, but yet sometimes hilarious quest, takes you from the glitz and glamour of the fashionable London restaurant scene to the wild, untamed tropical forests surrounding the Cardamom mountains region of Southeast Asia, as the participants race to discover the whereabouts of a remarkable plant and locate a misplaced family.

FOSSILS

Enjoy the hilarious antics of an elderly four-piece band as they embark on a whirlwind tour of several countries in Southeast Asia, unaware of their amazing worldwide success. The four musicians are inadvertently united and form a band named Fossils, whose unique sound filled an auditory hiatus lacking for decades in the modern day music industry. Pursued and hounded by ruthless record producers, this unassuming rock band discovers a new, exciting and carefree way of life, which they enjoy to the fullest, or at least what remains of it.

Viagra, snuff, and Rock 'n' Roll.

THE GOBS

Hoist up the incontinence pants, brush the fluff from your slippers, make a nice cup of cocoa, and enjoy... Because...THEY'RE BACK!

The Wrinkled Rockers return for their second hilarious action-packed adventure with : A sensational new album in production: A bird watching tour that goes horribly wrong: A devious duo returns seeking revenge: A flatulent Spook and a perilous rescue attempt in a foreign, but familiar, country.

What is there not to love?

Grab a copy of Fossils 2, before they get too old for this shit.

FROM BRITAIN WITH LOVE - Hilarious Comedy Saga
Fossils and The Gob's. together in **One Great Novel**

PATH – PARANORMAL ASSISTED TREASURE HUNTERS
Return of the Reich

A team of three psychics use their unique talents to provide a link between the mortal world and the celestial plane. Commissioned by lost souls; they find lost treasures for the troubled spirits, which they give to the mortal beneficiaries. One particular case finds the team caught up in a plot that had been conceived during world war two, which is instigated in the present day. The team has to solve a mystery that threatens to split the delicate fabric joining the two worlds.

NEXT – PATH 2
Covenant of the Gods

With the fate of humankind resting on their shoulders, the PATH team, along with the mortal Keepers and Guides around the world, are sent on various quests. Each test will push them all to their limits as time slowly ticks down towards Armageddon and their destiny.

RATCHET & STENCH – ANIMAL SLEUTHS
Dog Gone Mystery

When Cruft's Best of Breeds Champion mysteriously disappears; the finger of suspicion points at the owner of a rival kennel.

Somerset police find the missing Scottish terrier's dermal tracker but cannot find further evidence of a crime. Having no proof they are unable to do anything and drop any investigations.

The other dogs call in Ratchet and Stench, and even though

they uncover clues that suggest a brutal murder, the animal sleuths aren't convinced.

Non Fiction

DIABETES TYPE 2 – HELP SAFELY LOWER YOUR BLOOD SUGAR WITH THE TREE OF LIFE

This book is not written by Physicians or anyone with Ph.D.'s, but by medically trained diabetics who stumbled across pills capsules and powders made from the leaves and seeds of the Moringa tree. Dubbed The Miracle Tree or The Tree of Life. They found it reduced their blood sugar levels. This prompted research into this remarkable tree and its health benefits, which you will find outstanding. The tree grows in many parts of the world and indigenous people have been using its health giving properties for generations.

Moringa pills, capsules, and powders are now readily available worldwide, This publication will tell you about the research gained and the benefits to diabetics, along with Moringa's other health benefits. It will let you know current suppliers, and where you can research for yourself this amazing tree. It will also tell you how to grow organically for yourself and a few simple recipes you can use to enjoy the health benefits of Moringa.

SOMETHING TO READ WHILE TRAVELLING – THAILAND

Is an informative and entertaining companion to accompany you on your travels, which contains useful information about Thailand, some of which you won't find in travel guidebooks. While comprehensive travel guides will go into more detail on specific areas of Thailand; this publication will only briefly explain about popular tourist hotspots, giving you plenty of time to read and enjoy the Useful Tips: Thai Language Made Simple: Popular Thai Recipes: Fun Quizzes and Brainteasers:

Hilarious Jokes: Short Stories: and the full comedy adventure novel, SIAM STORM – A Thailand Adventure.

Leave your cares and woes at the arrivals section of the airport. Make sure you pack a big smile and this travelling companion in your suitcase. Open your heart and mind, and enjoy your wonderful time in the Land of Smiles.

****

If you enjoyed this novel, would you please be kind enough to write a review on Amazon or Goodreads, or to link it on Facebook or Twitter. In the digital age, such expressions of a readers satisfaction make a big difference to independent authors who cannot draw on the support of a giant publishing company's marketing. Many thanks.

Home Pages :
Amazon-http://www.amazon.com/Robert-A.-Webster/e/B004ZK975K
itunes-https://itunes.apple.com/us/artist/robert-a.-webster/id376017369?mt=11
Websites:
http://www.buddhasauthor.com/
http://stormwriter.weebly.com/
https://www.stormwriter.net/
connect:
Facebook-https://www.facebook.com/Buddhasauthor
Twitter-https://twitter.com/buddhasauthor